William Robinson

God's Acre Beautiful

The cemeteries of the future

William Robinson

God's Acre Beautiful
The cemeteries of the future

ISBN/EAN: 9783337405939

Printed in Europe, USA, Canada, Australia, Japan

Cover: Foto ©Andreas Hilbeck / pixelio.de

More available books at **www.hansebooks.com**

GOD'S ACRE BEAUTIFUL

or

The Cemeteries of the Future

W. Robinson, F.L.S.

LONDON

The Garden Office

37 Southampton Street, Covent Garden

NEW YORK

Scribner and Welford

1880

" Vermibus erepti puro consumimur igni
Indocte vetitum mens renovata petit."

"Why should we seek to clothe death with unnecessary terror, and spread horrors round the tomb of those we love? The grave should be surrounded with everything that might ensure tenderness and veneration."—WASHINGTON IRVING.

CONTENTS.

APPENDIX.

LIST OF PAGE ILLUSTRATIONS.

THE CEMETERIES OF THE FUTURE:

PERMANENT, UNPOLLUTED, INVIOLATE.

—◦—

THE sanitary reasons for preferring urn-
burial are admitted to be many and strong,
even by those who, for other reasons, are
not among its advocates. I propose to consider the subject from another point of view
altogether—the æsthetic one—or that of the
beauty of nature and art, which an improved
system of burial would make possible in all
that relates to the resting-place of the dead.
Many are apt to consider cremation as
meaning the absence of all the forms of

B

respect we usually bestow on this; and finally, of such associations as are generally gathered round the spot. But it is, on the contrary, the present system of burial which is open to the greatest objections in this respect. The history of many graveyards in crowded cities is this: Comparatively few years' accumulation of bodies, say from one to two generations, then finally closing from overcrowding. A generation or two passes away; many changes occur among those interested in preserving the graves, and soon their voice is heard no more in the matter. Then, at the will of some one or more persons desirous of disposing of a place which, frequently, is extremely valuable, at any moment the remains of every person buried therein are liable to be subjected to the utmost degradation; to be carted away as secretly as may be by some contractor, whose only object is to find a convenient shoot for them. Such changes are not unfrequent in London, though they are usually carried out as quietly as possible.* That secrecy, however, is not always exercised in operations of this kind is evident, from the fact that the remains from a disused cemetery in the west-central district of London,

---

* DESECRATION OF CITY GRAVEYARDS.—Are we not becoming too much accustomed to the idea that anything, however sacred, may be turned into money? Is not this the case with regard to burial-grounds? They fetch a large sum and they disappear. After the Great Fire of London care appears to have 'been taken in rebuilding the City to reserve in the main the burial-grounds of the parishes in which the churches themselves were not rebuilt. They are dotted as green spots all over the City, as many must often have observed. When the present extensive buildings of the Bank of England were erected, one whole parish was swallowed up. It was generally understood that its churchyard was respected, and is represented by the pleasant open garden court which gives such cheerfulness to the offices around it. St. Clement Danes' parish appears to view the subject in another light, and makes short work of the matter. Some years ago one of its

were spread over a couple of acres of Kensington Gardens a few years ago.

In Paris the state of things is no better, as there the bones are taken out of the ground, and the headstones and other memorials often destroyed within a few years of their being placed in position.

In America, owing to the extent of the beautiful cemeteries now existing near the larger cities, such evils are not so apparent,

burial-grounds, situate in Portugal Street, was disposed of for the site of part of King's College Hospital, and all trace of its former use has now disappeared. We have just heard that it has parted with another of its burial-grounds, adjoining Clement's Inn, for the site of a portion of the New Law Courts. One burial-ground, its principal one, in the middle of which the church of St. Clement Danes stands, still remains to the parish. An effort is being made, in connection with the Law Courts, to induce the parishioners to sell this also. Can we hope, after what has been done, that they will be proof against it? I trust we may. Sites can be got without invading these small churchyards, which have been bought over and over again by those who lie in them.—W. B., in *Times*.

though they exist there also. No matter how large cemeteries are, they are certain, in time, to have serious drawbacks from the conditions inherent to the present mode of burial. Under this system, the whole area of the place must, sooner or later, be filled with bodies; and must, eventually, be closed, unless in very sparsely-peopled districts. The small cemeteries in a city like London disappear from time to time, as noted above. The park-like ones in America may seem more secure from violation; but every future generation cannot, as the present one, enclose many hundreds of acres of valuable ground for burials. The American way is more decent than what is usual in France, but the difficulties of space alone would make it, if not impossible, a difficult plan to follow in the future.

PERMANENT AND BEAUTIFUL CEMETERIES
POSSIBLE WITH URN-BURIAL.

With any inoffensive and prompt system of reducing the body to ashes, this drawback of our burial system at once disappears. The ground not being occupied with bodies, there is no need to close the cemetery at any time. In graveyards of the size of the present overcrowded London ones, urn-burial could be carried on for hundreds of years without the slightest offence to the living. By the common consent of mankind "God's acre" is most fittingly arranged as a garden; and as the place for urn-burials need not occupy more than a fourth of the space of a large cemetery, the whole central or main part would be free space for gardens and groves of trees. The cemetery of the future must not only be a garden in the best sense of the word, but the most beautiful and best cared-for of all gardens. But as the present way of using the ground often leaves no room for either garden or planting, it may be best first to consider the subject in relation to monumental art, and to the dismal regiments of stones which cover the soil of our graveyards.

It is impossible to over-rate the opportunities for improvement in all that concerns the beauty or even the sentiment of the matter, which would be secured by the condition of *permanence*. Apart altogether from the closing of the burying-place, the decay from exposure, which now defaces memorial stones, is a very serious drawback. So recent a headstone record even as that of Gilbert White, in Selborne churchyard, is found with difficulty by the stranger; and many memorials erected in London cemeteries during the past fifty years are now crumbling to dust. There is no reason why these stone records should not be at least as enduring and as legible as the paper ones within the church. Most persons will agree that it is desirable that they should be so; now they are the very image of decay. While long duration is not possible under our present system, with urn-burial the simplest stone inscription may be in as good order a thousand years hence as to-day. With it also there would be a satis-factory realisation of the meaning conveyed by the word cemetery—a resting-place, or place of sleep, for the dead.

THE PRESENT GRAVEYARD NOT A PLACE OF REST.

The ordinary city graveyard being now only of temporary use, such monuments as

it possesses share the general fate of all
the other materials when it is closed. The
frequent disturbance of the ground for interments is against any good work in such art
as the place invites. In a London cemetery, such as that on the high road near the
Marble Arch (St. George's, Hanover Square),
it may be noticed that the memorial stones
are crumbling away, although this is one
of the best cared-for of closed cemeteries.
One cannot regret the poverty of the
"art" displayed in such places to decay and
be forgotten. In Paris the foundations of
roads are made of headstones only a few
years erected; and though in London memorial stones, erected to "perpetuate" the
memory of persons, are not cleared away
so promptly, the result in the end is very
much the same. Pieces of broken monumental stones, some of them bearing dates,

were among the débris for which a contractor found a convenient place in a
London public park. The effect of the
tombs and stones dotted thickly over
crowded city cemeteries is as ugly as it can
well be, but it is in accord with the very
temporary interest which, in the nature of
things, these places have for the public.

Notwithstanding the great attention and
vast and unselfish expense devoted by the
American people to their cemeteries, this
passage, from Oliver Wendell Holmes,
points to the fact that the same evils exist
there :—

The most accursed act of vandalism ever
committed within my knowledge was the uproot-
ing of the ancient gravestones in three, at least,
of our city burial-grounds, and one, at least, just
outside the city, and planting them in rows to
suit the taste for symmetry of the perpetrators.
The stones have been shuffled about like chess-

men, and nothing short of the Day of Judgment
will tell whose dust lies beneath any of those
records, meant by affection to mark one small
spot as sacred to some cherished memory.
Shame! shame! shame!—that is all I can say.
It was on public thoroughfares, under the eye of
authority, that this infamy was enacted. I
should like to see the gravestones which have
been disturbed or removed, and the ground
levelled, leaving the flat tombstones; epitaphs
were never famous for truth, but the old reproach
of "Here *lies*" never had such a wholesale illus-
tration as in these, outraged burial-places, where
the stone does lie above, and the bones do not
lie beneath.

NOBLE AND ENDURING ART MADE POSSIBLE
THROUGH URN-BURIAL.

By the adoption of urn-burial all that
relates to the artistic embellishment of a
cemetery would be at once placed on a very
different footing. One of the larger burial-
grounds now closed, perforce, in a less time

than that of an ordinary life, would accommodate a like number of burials on an improved system for many ages. The neglect and desecration of the resting-place of the dead inherent to the present system would give place to unremitting and loving care, for the simple reason that each living generation would be as much interested in the preservation of the cemetery as those that had gone before were at any previous time in its history. We should at once have, what is so much to be desired from artistic and other points of view—a permanent resting-place for our dead. With this would come the certainty that any memorials erected to their memory would be carefully preserved in the coming years, and free from the sacrilege and neglect so often seen. Hence an incentive to art which might be not unworthy of such places. The know-

ledge that our cemeteries would be sacred—
would be sacred to all, and jealously preserved by all, through the coming generations—would effect much in this new field for
artistic effort. In days when careful attention
is bestowed upon the designs of trifling details of our houses, it is to be hoped that we
shall soon be ashamed of the present state of
what should be the beautiful and unpolluted
rest-garden of all that remains of those
whom we have known, or loved, or honoured
in life, or heard of in death as having lived
not unworthy of their kind.

In endeavouring now to obtain any good
effects, defeat is certain through the essential conditions of the present mode of burial.
With urn-burial everything we can desire
for the artist is not only possible but easily
attained. Soft, green, undisturbed lawns;
stately and beautiful trees in many forms;

ground undisturbed, except in certain small parts; a background of surrounding groves; no hideous vistas of crowded stones; and the certainty that the monumental work done may remain permanently. And these are not all of the advantages which another system of burial would give us from the point of view of monumental art. The adoption of cremation does not necessarily do away with the tombs. So far from that, in old Roman cemeteries beautiful tombs may yet be seen, with the urns within them in as good order as when placed there two thousand years ago. In such cases a single tomb served as a family burial-place. The expense which is now spread over a variety of graves, headstones, and the purchase of ground, would, intelligently applied, build a tomb which might endure for ages. To make it beautiful and endur-

IN POMPEII—TOMBS USED FOR URNS.

ing as man and stone could, would be an aim not unworthy of an artist. A single burial in such an urn-tomb need not be so expensive as one in the commonest of the graves with which such large areas in our cities are now covered. The disturbance of the ground would not be necessary, as it is now; not to speak of the abolition of other onerous charges. The question of space is settled by the fact that one hundred of the simplest forms of urn could be placed in the space necessary for the burial of a single body in the ordinary way.

UGLINESS ABOLISHED AND INSCRIPTIONS AND MEMORIALS PRESERVED FROM DECAY.

The need for headstones would be done away with at once by urn-burial, inasmuch as it would lead to burials in columbaria, which are, in fact, large urn-tombs. In

many of them in Italy may still be seen
exposed the little urns containing human
ashes, dating from before the time of our era,
in as perfect preservation as if placed there
only a few days ago! Witness, for example,
the marvellously well-preserved columbaria
on the Vigna Codini and Via Aurelia.
With our present system no trace now
remains of some cemeteries in active, and
as was supposed "permanent," use a few
generations ago. The design of these
columbaria or tomb-temples would be worthy
of the best efforts of the architect, and their
formation in the most lasting and noble
form would not be so costly as the system
of deep burial of the body, the headstones,
and the continual and laborious moving of
the ground. These buildings would save all
memorials from destruction through exposure. This saving of all inscriptions and

memorials of the dead from the ravages
of time and weather is in itself a precious
gain, which no one will undervalue who
thinks of the importance of such records
in legal and other questions of public or private interest.* Buildings, sacred or otherwise, may be adapted for urn-burial. The
massive walls which should surround cemeteries might be formed into a covered way,
or series of covered ways, in which urn-
burial might be carried out.

* The external history of the Etruscans, as there are
no native chronicles extant, is to be gathered only from
scattered notices in Greek and Roman writers. Their
internal history, till of late years, was almost a blank ; but
by the continual accumulation of fresh facts it is now daily
acquiring form and substance, and promises ere long to be
as distinct and palpable as that of Egypt, Greece, or
Rome. . . . We are indebted for most of this knowledge
not to musty records drawn from the oblivion of centuries,
but to monumental remains—purer founts of historical
truth—landmarks which, even when few and far between,
are the surest guides across the expanse of distant ages—

ALL RELIGIOUS OR BEAUTIFUL
CEREMONY EASY.

Inasmuch as no ceremony, sacred or otherwise, need be omitted in the mode of burial here advocated, so there would be fitting opportunities for the building of such religious structures as might be thought desirable in each case. When we come to the ceremony of urn-burial itself, we find it one that needs by no means be repulsive. The simplest urn ever made for the ashes of a Roman soldier is far more beautiful

to the monuments which are still extant on the sites of the ancient cities of Etruria, or have been drawn from their cemeteries, and are stored in the museums of Italy and of Europe. The internal history of Etruria is written on the mighty walls of her cities, and on other architectural monuments, on her roads, her sewers, her tunnels, but above all in her sepulchres; it is to be read on graven rocks, and on the painted walls of tombs; but its chief chronicles are inscribed on *stelæ* or tombstones, on sarcophagi and cinerary urns.—Dennis, *Cities and Cemeteries of Etruria.*

than the costly funeral trappings used in the most imposing burial pageant of modern times. Of urns of a more ambitious kind, the variety and the beauty are often remarkable, as may be seen in our national and various private collections. It would be a gain to art if some of the money spent on coffins, which rot unseen in the earth, were devoted to such urns, which do not decay, and which might be placed in the light of day, and perhaps teach a lesson in art as well as bear a record. There is a square-sided marble urn in the Woburn collection, with simple carving of the shoots of the common ivy over it, which is more suggestive of all that is beautiful in a memorial than any elaborate effort in a modern cemetery.

The ceremony of burial in this way, too, how different it may be made from that with which we are familiar! What a contrast

there is between that picture of the noble
Roman woman, surrounded by her maidens
and friends, herself bearing her husband's
ashes to the tomb, and the black array,
the paid, half-besotted, mutes, and the
hideous box in which the remains of poor
humanity are nailed up for a decay as needless as it is odious, to any one who has seen
it or thought of it.   What a gain it would
be to get rid of much of this Monster
Funereal, the most impudent of the ghouls
that haunt the path of progress!   Vulgar
show may, of course, be indulged in as much
one way as the other; but it is pleasant to
think of the ugly things and trades that may
be abolished in cities when urn-burial became practicable.   No doubt simplicity is
possible, and is sometimes practised as far
as may be, with the present system; but with
urn-burial certain main causes of expenditure

MARBLE, PORPHYRY, AND TERRA-COTTA CINERARY URNS AND CHESTS,
DRAWN FROM SPECIMENS IN THE BRITISH MUSEUM.

and show may be abolished altogether—
great difficulties of transport being one of
them.* Given a crematorium near the
town, and transport to the cemetery, however distant, involves little trouble. To a
people scattered over the world, like our
own, the ease with which remains could be
brought from any distant country, without
inconvenience, and at little cost, to its final
resting-place at home, deserves consideration.

* I am speaking now of sentimental reasons, and I
adduce a second, which first called my own attention to
the unpleasant consequences which arise from our present
system. It has been my misfortune to lose four of my
nearest relations in different parts of the world. It has been
also a subject of regret to me that their remains lie so far
off. I care little for the fate which happens to their bodies
—and yet, had such a practice as Cremation been in use,
it would sometimes have been a comfort to feel that I had
their ashes with me. Collected in an urn, they might
either repose in columbaria, like those at Rome, or in a
mortuary chapel in my own house.—The Rev. Brooke
Lambert.

BURIALS IN AND AROUND CHURCHES AND PUBLIC BUILDINGS MIGHT BE PRACTISED TO ANY EXTENT.

In connection with this part of the subject, it may be well to consider the opportunities which urn-burial would afford for depositing the inoffensive remains of the dead in our churches—old and new. It would have the great advantage of permitting burials to be carried out in churches and city graveyards to any extent, and for any number of years. For various reasons, many persons would prefer burial in churches or near them; but, as is well-known, the evils of the present system of burial became so horrible and so evidently dangerous in the case of city graveyards and churches, that burial within cities had to be forbidden by law, and not too soon. The

state of things from which extra-mural burial
saved us are again appearing in populous
suburban districts. At Highgate, for example, strong undertakers' men have been
made seriously ill while at work by the
underflowing drainage from the higher parts
of the burial-ground.* At no distant day,
under the present system, the numerous
family tombs and graves in our extensive
suburban cemeteries must fall into disuse.
As extra-mural burial was not made law
in London only, but in other large cities

* Communications have reached us, and observations
been made, which compel us to draw serious attention to
the condition of some of the cemeteries within the metropolitan district, which are rapidly becoming sources of peril
not only to the neighbourhoods in which they are situated,
but to the whole metropolis. The emanations from some
of the newly-opened graves is so horribly offensive as to
occasion nausea among those who attend at funerals. As
cases of actual illness, after being present at interments in
some of the cemeteries, have occurred, there can be no
doubt about the danger. Meanwhile the crowding of the

throughout the United Kingdom, it was a most radical change. Families who had for generations been buried in city churchyards have now to take their dead without the walls. Urn-burial would change all this. Establish this system, and people who have family-tombs in our neglected city graveyards would begin to take a renewed interest in them, an interest that might save them from the desecration so often mentioned. It would tend to make our churches more interesting, and even our cities, for there is

graves is apparent. The number of bodies laid in the earth may not be excessive when calculated upon the whole acreage of the space licensed, but with an eye to the future the ground seems to be appropriated in parcels, while in some of the older cemeteries there is really no room for more graves, and the licence ought to be withdrawn. This is a matter of so much concern to the health of the community that we forbear to run the risk of weakening the evidence of facts by any comment. The intervention of the Secretary of State should not be delayed.—*Lancet*, September 27, 1879.

a certain fitness in men resting in death near the scene of their life and labours. The ashes of those who had deserved well of their country might be brought home from any distant place where they had perished, and receive a place of honour in our national churches or buildings. Our great dead now, very properly, find a resting-place in Westminster Abbey, and there is no reason whatever why other great cities or other parts of the country should not have the same system for their own most worthy sons. But you cannot long have a place of horror and a place of honour too, and therefore urn-burial makes this public honour of the memory of the great dead to any extent, and for all time, not only possible but easy. Urn-burial is, in view of the change it would cause in this and in other ways, worthy in all its bearings of the serious consideration of the clergy. In the cemeteries of the future, of which a slight outline will be given further on, buildings will have to be formed for the reception of the memorials of the dead. In our churches these already exist, and would, for a long time, have the advantage over all others. Vaults, passages, niches, and walls, would form suitable places for urns, and their accompanying inscriptions or memorials. In new or old churches, when these places were insufficient, portions of the building could be constructed for this purpose, which, being in complete harmony with the object and associations of religious buildings, would tend to encourage good architectural and artistic work. And not the church only, but the surrounding space would be valuable for the same reason. It is well to remember that some of the more beautiful tombs to be seen in modern cemeteries are based on ancient models of tombs, used as depositories for urns. Such family tombs would probably be built in our now disused churchyards; they might be above ground, and they would involve no disturbance of the earth, as the present grave-burials do, and little or no interference with trees or planting.

CEMETERIES BEAUTIFUL AND PERMANENT PUBLIC GARDENS.

Apart from the question of art is the important consideration of the great advantages the improved system would give us in adding natural beauty to the gardens of the dead, and improving many large open spaces in our cities of all sizes. Given a space equal to one of our largest London cemeteries, or one of those in America several hundred acres in extent, we may begin to outline what the cemetery of the future may easily be made. Permanent and inviolable it must be. The cemetery of the future not only prevents the need of occupying large areas of ground with decaying bodies, in a ratio increasing with the population and with time, but leaves ample space to spare for those open green lawns, without which no good natural effect is possible in such places. It is to be a national garden in the best sense ; safe from violation as the *via sacra*, and having the added charms of pure air, trees, grass, and flowers. The open central lawns should always be preserved from the follies of the geometrical and stone gardeners, so as to secure freedom of view and air, and a resting-place for the eye.

THE CEMETERY OF THE FUTURE:
BUILDINGS.

Approaching the boundary, but not quite near it, should be erected a covered way, as strong and lasting as rock. This is to form a series of urn-receptacles on its inner side, well but simply designed with the best architectural skill obtainable. This alone, in the case of a large place, could easily be arranged to afford space for burials for ages. All other tombs, and buildings of whatever kind, should be confined to a belt of the ground within and near the covered way, and, with their accompanying groves, should not occupy more than a fourth of the whole space. The covered way should not be the work of one man or period, and this being so, it would be well to separate its parts by planting or otherwise—the division

occurring, if possible, in places commanding
views of the surrounding country.

We are now considering a cemetery of
the largest size and first importance — a
national or metropolitan one. Several
reasons determine that the covered way
and main buildings shall not be on the
extreme boundary ; namely, to have them
in as quiet a position as possible, as safe
from injury on their outer as on their
inner sides : to secure freedom from any
kind of nuisance which might arise, from the
buildings being placed too near property
over which the governing body of the cemetery had no control ; also to allow of the
buildings being screened from the surrounding neighbourhood by tall trees, on any side
where the views were not such as would add
to the landscape beauty of the place.

Thus it would be possible to control the

views not only from the centre to the
covered way and tombs, and *vice versâ*, but
also beyond them, and to secure freedom
from any objectionable sights or sounds.
The actual boundary would be secured in
a more ordinary but effectual manner.
There being ample space within and without
the great covered way and accompanying
tombs for much noble tree-planting, the
larger trees need not be planted near tombs,
as there have been many instances of the
disturbance of these by their roots. The
buildings should be near and between groves
of evergreens, and the dwarfer flowering,
weeping, or columnar trees. These would
partly conceal and soften them, as seen from
the central parts. A main walk passes by
these groves and the monuments, and it
should be the principal, and if possible the
only, road in the place. A beautiful church

or classic temple, such as that at Munich,
might form the entrance; this and all other
structures being built subject to the approval
of a group of artists and architects who
would see that their design and workman-
ship were not unworthy of the spot.

FREE AND SIMPLE BURIALS FOR THE POOR.

Some might claim the privilege of erecting urn-temples or other buildings for public
use, or for securing free urn-burial to the
poor who desired it. It may be easily
shown that urn-burial is much the less costly
way, and those who have to combat the
prejudices against it must take care that
it is made as inexpensive as possible.
Moreover, as it is desirable that no person,
however poor or friendless, who desires it
should be denied for pecuniary reasons this

mode of burial, so there should be free burials for the very poor—free from any demeaning condition.* Although the plan of this paper is to deal with only certain of the aspects of the question, not commonly considered, a very sad one which many must notice is that of the cruel sufferings of the poor owing to the ordinary system of burial. Few but those who go among them much, know the hardships to which they are reduced through the death of the head, of the breadwinner, or other working member of the family. This is frequently preceded by the exhaustion of all the little means of the house, wholly derived, perhaps, from the labour of the one who lies dead. Then come these excessive burial and funeral

* The mode of burying paupers in London and Paris is an abomination and a disgrace. In London, as may be seen by reference to the Appendix for the account of the Tooting Cemetery, it is a public danger as well as a horror.

charges, which often cannot be met; or, if met, absorb the last shilling in the house. A case was some time ago reported in the daily papers where an undertaker in London allowed a body to lie in the house till the police had to interfere, because the widow could not advance him the whole of the sum of eight pounds. Proportionate charges for the most useless and hideous of all forms of display are too well known in every rank; and cases such as the above are not uncommon in our towns, though seldom reported in the newspapers.*

* BOW STREET.—AN UNBURIED BODY. A poor woman named Laller applied to Mr. Vaughan on Tuesday, and stated that on Monday week her son had died. He was nineteen years old. The body was taken to an undertaker named France, who lived at 9 Great White Lion Street, Seven Dials, who agreed to bury it for £3 : 3s. She paid him £2 : 10s., but could not at present make up the remainder. The man France had made her sign a paper by which it was agreed that he need not bury the body unless the whole of the money was paid, and as she could

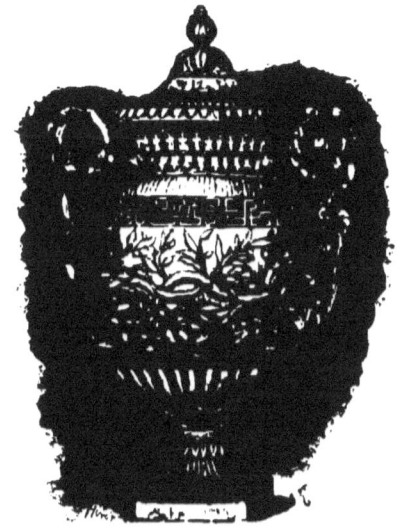

From the Museum of the Vatican.

SYLVAN AND FLORAL BEAUTY
OF THE CEMETERY.

The sylvan charms of such a spot might
be greater than is usually obtained in public

not pay the 13s. the body still remained unburied. She
had received only about £1 : 5s. Mr. Mitchell said the
parish were quite willing to bury the body, but they had
wanted the case to come before a magistrate first, as this
was not the first case of the kind against this man France.
He had been at this court and at Marlborough Street
several times for not burying bodies.

gardens. The protecting architectural wall is far enough from the boundary to allow of groves of oak and other hardy native trees being planted outside it; these groves to have grass and wild and naturalised flowers beneath and between them. The interior groves and gardens might be the home of all the beautiful green things that grow in our climate. The main portion of the surface being always free for such ends, we should soon have a beautiful tree-garden which might even be of great public use. As some might desire to enrich the place with useful buildings, so others might claim to plant memorial trees or groups, where the opportunity existed. The views should be numerous and carefully considered. The planting should be wholly natural, in the best sense of the word. The outer portion, with its bordering tombs, columbaria, archi-

tectural covered way, and churches, should
contain all the purely artistic adornments of
the place; while the central portions should
be quite free from the drill-master manner
of marshalling plants, and sundry like effects
of a too prevalent style of gardening.

However all-sufficient the sylvan charms
of the place might be, a desirable structure,
in a bad climate like ours, would be the
winter-garden, in which religious or burial
ceremonies could take place at inclement
seasons—in an agreeable temperature, and
in the midst of a variety of beautiful living
things. Few would object to this plan were
it not from the objectionable way in which
such structures are generally designed, the
too frequent idea being that a glass shed
more or less vast is the best plan. But
the palm-house in the Edinburgh botanic
garden, and a variety of structures used as

winter gardens in continental cities, prove
that vegetation thrives in buildings with
stately and solid walls. Far more beautiful
effects are obtained in such, from the contrast of the graceful forms of palms and
other fine plants with noble building, than
in the ordinary way. The temperature
necessary to keep plants from temperate
climes in health, would be also that which
would make it agreeable to people assisting
at ceremonies, for which, of course, its most
important spaces should be reserved.

CREMATORIUM, OR ANY STRUCTURE AN-
SWERING A LIKE END, BEST SEPARATED
FROM THE CEMETERY.

As no body in a state of decay should
ever enter into our garden-cemetery, the
process of cremation, or any improvement
on it, may be carried out elsewhere. But

where, as will no doubt often be the case, the crematorium is constructed on the spot, it will be best to separate it from the general scene by planting or buildings. There is no reason why such a building should be so planned that any of its arrangements need offend the most sensitive person. There is no reason why any rite or act to be performed therein should not be carried out in accordance with due respect to every feeling of the friends of a deceased person. One of the earliest impediments in the way of improvement will probably be the failure to give due weight to these considerations in plans of crematoria. It need scarcely be said that such a building should only be erected under the supervision of an architect of proved good taste and care.

An important result of the change herein advocated would be the preservation, as public gardens, of the many large cemeteries now in use, because with urn-burials continually going on they would remain inviolate. Their fate when filled and finally closed is, as before shown, very doubtful.

IMPROVEMENT IN PLANTING OLD GRAVEYARDS.

Apart from the question of improvement in burial, the present state of our rural cemeteries may be fittingly alluded to here. Possessing often considerable advantages as to site and soil, and associations that always seem to call for some care in adorning them with trees and flowers, they are often seen amidst our fairest landscapes as bare as a stoneyard, and, as regards vegetation, much less interesting than the hedgerows by which they are surrounded. The church-garden, even if small, need never be arid or

IN A GARDEN CEMETERY.

ugly. But if there were only the walls—so
often hard and naked—they alone might form
a garden. Fresh foliage and blossoms are not
often seen to greater advantage than against
the worn stones of our churches, often un-
adorned with even ivy or Virginian creeper.
Many of the best climbing roses and other
climbers may be grown well on these walls.
The several sides of the church might each
have the plants suitable to their shelter or
position. The walls round graveyards
might also offer a suitable position for
numerous low-climbing plants and bushes.
Tombs may be partially garlanded with
trailers, sweetbriar, or honeysuckle, and all
this without disturbance of the ground or
stones. It is best to adorn or grace-
fully relieve, instead of obliterating, such
objects. The ground is generally well
adapted for trees, and even the turf itself

may be converted into a garden of early flowers. Indeed, the graveyard might often be a tree-garden, and one not without its uses. In planting it is essential not to hide the building from important points of view; too much care can hardly be paid to the views obtainable towards or from the site.

In cities and large towns trees often embellish the space round the churches to a much larger extent than in the rural districts, though the practice of planting evergreens in city churchyards is a foolish one in all ways, as they can only perish under our smoke plague. In such cases the summer-clad trees only should be used. Our old city churchyards could all be easily converted into oases of trees. The not unusual way of levelling or removing the headstones, and making the whole into a formal garden, is not the best. There is no real need for any sacrilege of the kind. The trees that flourish in such places are those that require little preparation of the ground —weeping and other native trees. Much short-lived and formal flower-gardening should be avoided, in consequence of the ceaseless care and cost it requires; the attention should mainly be devoted to the suitable hardy trees.

PRIVATE BURIAL-PLACES.

Near country seats urn-burial would lead to the family burial-place within the grounds —a quiet inclosed glade in some sunny spot, chosen for its beauty, embowered in a grove of evergreens, the grass sprinkled with hardy native or naturalised flowers only—so as to prevent any frequent attention on the part of workmen. Such a spot, with its carpet of turf, and walls of musical-leaved trees, wholly

free from the long-lasting and many-staged
horror of decomposition, which makes the
ordinary churchyard so far from inviting to
many persons, would form a fitting place of
meditation for the living, as well as of repose
for the ashes of the dead.

COUNTRY CEMETERIES.

The drawbacks of various kinds known
to exist in connection with large urban
cemeteries, are often supposed not to exist
in the case of rural ones; but, unhappily,
they are sometimes in quite as bad a state
as those in cities. Overcrowding is far
from uncommon in country districts, but
here there is less chance of the wholesale
removals before mentioned. Some years
ago, however, when certain changes in the
church required the raising of a number of
bodies in the churchyard at Cobham, in

CYPRESS GROVE IN PRIVATE CEMETERY.

Surrey, the work of the navvies was of the most horrible and dangerous character, and was accomplished with difficulty in the early mornings, partly under the influence of repeated doses of gin administered to the men. Such removals are not uncommon, but they are performed as secretly as possible, for fear of raising opposition. In many quiet country places there is as great need to close the graveyard as ever existed in large ones, and sometimes greater danger, owing to imperfect drainage. In such cases any improvements or changes are extremely difficult to carry out, owing to the state of the ground. The same plan already spoken of in connection with great urban or national cemeteries would be proportionately no less advantageous, on a small scale, for country towns and villages. Danger to the living; pollution of earth or water; overcrowding;

decay of memorials through exposure ; hideous ugliness of stone, telling of accumulated horrors beneath the turf—all these, and many other evils, should be avoided in country as in town, while the various advantages of the improved system would be as precious in one case as in the other. The church and its vaults, and other unused spaces, and a covered way, replacing the whole or a portion of the usual fence, would in most cases suffice for ages for urn-burial, leaving the whole of the churchyard itself free, as a beautifully planted spot. Urns placed under memorial windows, and in various positions on the walls, would invite monumental work of the highest class. The sentiment that people's ashes might repose in the church where they worshipped during life would not be interfered with in this case, whereas, frequently in rural districts nowadays, the present system compels the formation of a new graveyard away from the church.

"THE EARTH TO EARTH" SYSTEM.

The "earth to earth system," or the burial of the body without a more or less solid covering, has been much talked of as a substitute for the usual mode of burial. It has in reality no merits whatever. By coffinless burial our ugly and noisome cemeteries can in no sense be bettered. The ground is occupied in the same way. It is an advantage to dispense with the needless and more or less costly wooden or leaden envelopes, but it is a mistake to suppose that very rapid decay takes place through their absence, as it has been proved that bodies deeply buried without coffins often decay slowly in ordinary soils. But even if the action of decomposition were always as rapid as it is in some soils, burial without coffins in no way frees us from the serious responsibility of needlessly polluting earth, air, and water. All the drawbacks, all the horrors, all the dangers of the present system would be just the same with this proposed alternative, which is, indeed, worthy of no serious attention as a substitute for the usual mode of burial. It has not even the merit of being a safe system, and those responsible for the public health could not permit of its use in the case of persons dying from confluent smallpox and putrid fevers.

This earth to earth system, so called, is merely a recurrence to the old-fashioned English way of burial in a shroud of woollen or other material. There are many evidences of the commonness of this practice in our forefathers' time, and it is not on record that they were any less free from the evils

of the graveyard than ourselves. The
wholly odious use of leaden coffins is
defended by no one, not even the undertaker. Mr. Haden, who strenuously advocated the use of this old system, with, as
some have thought, the needless addition of
basket-coffins, has dealt with this question in
an ugly utilitarian way, which will, it is to
be hoped, commend itself to few, and certainly to no one who has a particle of the
feeling which animated the old Romans
when they took their very effective precautions against disturbance of, or insult to,
the ashes of their dead. It has been proved,
over and over again, that the saturation of
the soil by human remains is fraught with
the greatest danger to the public health.
We have it on the testimony of trustworthy
and scientific witnesses, embodied in reports
to Parliament, that disease on an extensive

E

scale has been traced directly to this systematic and extensive pollution of the ground with bodies, yet Mr. Haden has nothing better to offer us than further pollution of the same description.

Since, he says, it is impossible for nature to err, and since it may be taken as an axiom that she will ever be found ready to supply us with the means of doing that which she requires us to do, need we ever be at a loss for ground in which to bury our dead? If it be true that a body, properly buried, is resolved in five, or at most, six years, it follows that at that interval, or at intervals as much longer as we please, we may *bury again and again in the same ground, with no other effect than to increase its substance and to raise its surface.* Is there, however, no ground in the immediate neighbourhood of our own city that would be the better for this increase and for being thus raised? The cremationists will tell us that there is not, but is there the shadow of a foundation for such a statement? Along the course of our great river from London to the sea,

for instance, have we not vast lowland tracts of
rich alluvial soil deposited by that very river and
capable of being drained, planted, and beautified,
in which, with equal benefit to the land and to
ourselves, we may bury our dead for centuries?
If, as we have seen, the surface of the Holborn
Burial-ground was raised 15 feet or 18 feet by
the interments within it of three centuries, *why
should not the lowlands of Kent and Essex be
raised and reclaimed in the same way*, and as
much as possible of the valuable ground in
and about the city, now occupied as cemeteries,
be restored to better uses? What if it take us
thousands instead of hundreds of years thus to
reclaim and elevate such lands, and so practically dispose of our difficulties as to burial for
ever?

Anything more puerile and impracticable
could surely not be thought of or written by
any person who knows the state of our
graveyards and cemeteries, and has ever
desired their reform. In the " Report on

the Practice of Interment in Towns,"* pre-
sented to both Houses of Parliament, it is
stated that "there appear to be *no cases in
which emanations from human remains in an
advanced state of decomposition are not of a
deleterious nature;*" and yet Mr. Haden, in
the name of progress, seriously proposes to
raise and reclaim "*the lowlands of Kent and
Essex*" *with decaying human bodies!* He
knows that in the course of ages small
patches of ground in London and other
cities have been raised by piling them with
boxes containing bodies, and, accordingly,
proceeds to improve the home counties
agriculturally in the same wholesome way!
Happily our lowlands are not in want of any
such "improvement," which is all the more
singular as a suggestion from one who
poses as a teacher of graveyard reform and

* Clowes and Sons, Stamford Street, 1843.

æsthetics. Proof that the "earth to earth" plan is also unsound from sanitary and scientific points of view will be found in the Appendix.

BURYING REPEATEDLY IN THE SAME SOIL.

Official authorities, in opposing urn-burial, have maintained that in "good soil the body may be considered as decomposed and non-existent in from twenty to twenty-five years, and that the same spot may then be used again for the purpose of burying, precisely as if it were virgin soil." This was in reply to objections as to the great areas of land that must be used for this purpose. "No!" Mr. Holland replies, "the same land can be used at least four times in a century if it is 'good,'—is dry and well drained 'soil'" — a remarkable admission

from those who desire to respect or preserve their ancestors' dust! This system of
reburying in the same ground again is part
of Mr. Haden's pet plan, but what the feeling of the public is about all such plans is
shown in the following extract from a lecture
by the Rev. Brooke Lambert :—

"The results of the improvements in the Tamworth churchyard show me that, however little I
may be susceptible to what becomes of my own
remains, there is no subject on which people feel
more deeply than the disturbance of the remains
of their ancestors, and even the displacement of
effete memorials of them. From the letters of
the better class to the comments of the inhabitants of "Day's Yard," who wished that those
beneath would come up and punish me and my
Churchwardens, I find that the prevailing feeling
is that the dead ought never to be removed, nor
the position of their monuments changed even by
a hair's breadth. *Now whilst our present system of
burial remains, such changes in their places of interment must occur.*"

The system of removing the bodies after a lapse of years and burying in the same ground again is carried out in all its ugliness in the Paris cemeteries, but it is so evidently wrong from a sanitary point of view, and also from that of common decency, that it is to be hoped it will never be practised in this country, and it has no chance of success in America, where, more than in any country, the dead receive decent burial. What law, human or divine, justifies this ignoble disturbance of the remains of the dead, and the use of the ground for the burial of other bodies, to be in their turn disinterred in like manner ? One may see the effect of it in many exposed bones and skulls in Alpine and North Italian valleys, where thousands of acres of waste land lie around. It is no less offensive, and more dangerous, in large cities ; and those who advocate it

for our English cemeteries must indeed be
at the end of their arguments. Those who
know the revolting way the remains of all
not rich enough to pay for the ground in
"perpetuity" in French cemeteries will not
regret to learn that the Municipal Council
of that city have opened an important com-
petition, calculated to ascertain the most
prompt and inoffensive way of reducing the
body to its inoffensive parts, and thus eventually lead the way to a much needed reform.

ONE TRUE WAY TO BURIAL REFORM.

There is not, and there never can be,
any satisfactory system of disposing of the
dead, which does not do, as promptly and
as inoffensively as possible, what is now done
in the slowest and most horrible manner.
Until some better system is devised, crema-

tion is the only method which will rapidly resolve the body into its harmless elements by a process which cannot offend the living, and which shall render the remains of the dead innocuous. This system is also that which gives us the amplest opportunity for making "God's acre beautiful" a blessing instead of a danger to its neighbourhood; by its means we may have memorials preserved from decay; ground from sacrilege; soil and water from impurity; art not unworthy of its aim; church-burial for all who desire it; space for gardens and groves in our cemeteries; the mindfulness and care of each successive generation; deliverance from the undertaker, and his "effects;" many precious open spaces in cities free from dread or danger; age-enduring cemeteries, in which efforts towards "perpetuating" the memory of the dead need not be so delusory as they now are; quiet places, where the ashes of the dead should never be dishonoured, but might find unpolluted rest.

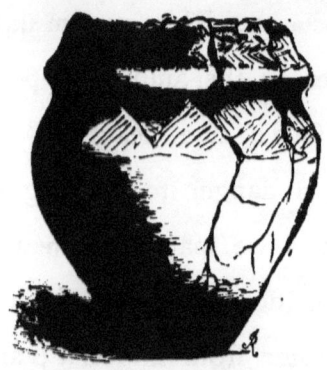

Irish Cinerary Urn—County Down.

THE MANAGEMENT AND CONTROL OF CEMETERIES.

Whatever the future of our cemeteries may be, it is much to be desired that they should not be controlled by trading companies. This is not the way the Americans have established their beautiful cemeteries, which are as well arranged and kept as is

possible under the present system of burial.
So large and so important a question as the
burial of the dead should never be in the
hands of those who merely regard it from
the point of view of money-making. It is
well known that the profits from certain
cemeteries in some of the pleasantest
suburbs of London are very large; the
temptation to continue burial in them, longer
than decency or sanitary reasons would permit, will probably lead to danger in the
future from pollution of air and water. The
present state of some of our cemeteries close
to London is already dangerous and offensive; on this point, Mr. S. Haden makes
some just remarks :—

Considering that our reason for discontinuing
intra-mural interment was that the soil of the old
city graveyards had become so saturated and
super-saturated with animal matter that it could

no longer properly be called soil, it might have
been supposed that, in establishing the new cemeteries, stringent provision would be made that
such a pollution of the ground should not again
occur; the more so that it must have been foreseen that, by the inevitable extension of the town,
the then suburban would become again the intra-
mural cemetery, and that the horrors of the old
graveyard would thus come to be repeated and
multiplied.   Not only was no such provision
made, but one of the chief of the new companies
gave prompt proof of its unfitness to comprehend
and to use the powers intrusted to it, by making
the extraordinary proposal to bury 1,335,000
bodies in seven acres of ground.   Here, since it
may not else be believed, is this amazing proposal :—" It has been found," say the newly
installed directors of the General Cemetery
Company (Kensal Green), in recommendation of
the plans which they are proposing for their
future guidance,—" it has been found that seven
acres will contain 133,500 graves; each grave
will contain ten coffins; thus, accommodation
will be found for 1,335,000 deceased paupers."
The very *naïveté* of this proposal might, one

would think, have at once opened the eyes and
excited the alarm of those who were conferring
on these companies almost unlimited powers, and
have prepared them for the abuse of those powers
which speedily followed. No such alarm, however, appears to have been excited, and a system
of interment founded, we must suppose, on this
surprising calculation, was at once inaugurated
and permitted. If, in the old graveyards, the
Vestries and Guardians of the poor saved themselves expense by piling coffin upon coffin till
the hole which they had dug would contain no
more, the new cemetery companies increased their
dividends and propitiated their shareholders by
doing precisely the same thing. It is surprising
that the Government, which refused to listen to
the recommendations of the Board of Health in
this matter, should have preferred to intrust the
sanitary interests of a great city, and so important a duty as the burial of its dead, to a
class of men who, however respectable, had shown
themselves ignorant of the very first principles
which should govern them in the management of
such things.

Again, apart from the improbability that a

mere trading company would prove itself competent to deal with so large, so technical, and so delicate a question as the burial of the dead, it might have been foreseen that the material interests of such a company, its obligations to its shareholders, and its trade associations, could never be in harmony with, but must ever be opposed to, the interests of the public.

The very different spirit with which the new cemeteries in America are undertaken by the leading citizens is well known to many who have travelled there. Cemeteries in America, as well as in Europe, are conducted on various plans. A number of them are under the control of the city authorities, and of course are seldom self-supporting. Others, again, are the property of religious communities, which sometimes manage to pay expenses, and have at times something left for the benefit of the church; but in these cases there is very little security

ENTRANCE TEMPLE COLUMBARIUM.

IN AMERICAN GARDEN CEMETERY.

to the owners of burial-places, for, the city
council or the trustees of the church may at
any time pass an ordinance for the removal
of the dead to other" quarters, particularly
if the burial-ground be situated in or near
a city and has become valuable for other
purposes. In that case the last resting-place
of the dead is easily condemned as a nuisance, and the consecrated ground is sold for
building purposes,·for the sake of gain ; and
in this way, as in our cities, the houses of the
living are erected over the graves of the dead.

The plan that has given the greatest
satisfaction to the public, and led to the
creation of the nobler cemeteries near all the
larger cities, and to many beautiful cemeteries in the Western States, and in remote
places, is that where every lot-holder is a
member of the corporation of the cemetery,
and where the entire income is devoted to

the improvement and perpetual care of the cemetery. Some of these bodies, in addition to forming garden and park-like cemeteries, to which the best in Paris and London are mere stone yards, have already accumulated a considerable surplus, and there is not the least doubt that in a few years they will have a fund the interest of which will be more than sufficient to keep the grounds perpetually in complete order.

The following extract is from the Act of Incorporation of the Spring Grove Cemetery at Cincinnati.

SECTION 6. This Corporation is authorised to purchase, or take by gift or devise, and hold land exempt from execution and from any appropriation to public purposes, for the sole purpose of a cemetery, not exceeding three hundred acres ; one hundred and sixty-seven acres of which, such as shall be designated by the directors, shall be exempt from taxation, and the remainder shall be

taxed as other lands, until the legislature shall otherwise direct.   After paying for such land, *all future receipts, whether from the sale of lots, from donations, or otherwise, shall be applied exclusively, under the direction of the board, to laying out, preserving, protecting, and embellishing the cemetery, and the avenues leading thereto; and to paying the necessary expenses of the Corporation.*

Marble Cinerary Urn—British Museum.

F

Large Glass Cinerary Urn, found at Southfleet, in Kent, now in British Museum

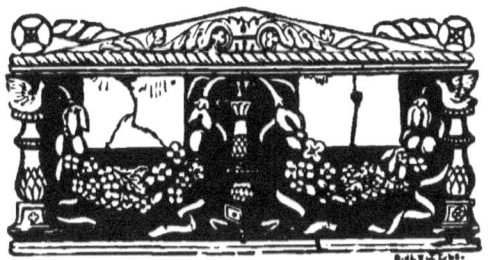

Urn in Clumber Collection—(White's *Worksop*).

APPENDIX.

As the preceding pages deal mainly with the æsthetic side of the burial question, the following are added for the convenience of those who wish to satisfy themselves as to other reasons for reform in our mode of burial.

BURIAL : A HORRIBLE PRACTICE.

If people could see the human body after the process of decomposition sets in, which is as soon as the vital spark ceases to exist, they would not want to be buried ; they would be in favour of cremation. If they could go into a dissecting-room and see the horrid sights of the dissecting-table, they would not wish to be buried. Burying the human body, I think, is a horrible thing. If more was known about the human frame while undergoing decomposition, people would turn with horror from the custom of burying their dead. It sometimes takes a human body fifty, sixty, eighty years—yes, longer than that—to decay. Think of it ! The remains of a friend lying under six feet of ground, or less, for that

length of time, going through the slow stages of decay,
and other bodies all this time being buried around these
remains. Infants grow up and pass into manhood or
womanhood; grow old and get near the door of death,
and during all that time the body which was buried in
their infancy lies a few feet underground in this sicken-
ing state, undergoing the slow process of decay. Think
of thousands of such bodies crowded into a few acres of
ground, and then reflect that these graves, or many of
them, in time fill with water, and that water percolates
through the ground and mixes with the springs and
wells and rivers from which we drink. Why, if people
knew what physicians know, what they have learned in
the dissecting-room, they would look upon burning the
human body as a beautiful art in comparison with
burying it. There is something eminently repulsive to
me about the idea of lying a few feet under ground for
a century, or perhaps two centuries, going through the
process of decomposition. When I die I want my body
to be burned. Any unprejudiced mind needs but little
time to reflect in forming a conclusion as to which is
the better method of disposing of the body. Common
sense and reason proclaim in favour of cremation.
There is no reason for keeping up the burial custom,
but many against it, some of the most practical of which
are but too recently developed to need mention. There
is nothing repulsive in the idea of cremation. People's
prejudice is the only opponent it has. If they could be
awakened to a sense of the horror of crowding thousands of bodies under the ground, to pollute in many
instances the air we breathe and the water we drink,

their prejudice would be overcome. Cremation would
be taken for what it truly is, a beautiful method of disposing of the body.—Dr. S. D. Gross.

PRECAUTIONS AS TO PROOF OF DEATH.

The only serious objection urged from any
quarter against the prompt and harmless reduc-
tion of the body to its inoffensive parts is that of
the supposed immunity it would give to poisoners ;
and this question is dealt with by Sir Henry
Thompson and Mr. Lavel of Paris.

It has been said, and most naturally, what guarantee
is there against poisoning if the remains are burned, and
it is no longer possible, as after burial, to reproduce the
body for the purpose of examination ?   It is to my mind
a sufficient reply that, regarding only " the greatest good
for the greatest number," the amount of evil in the shape
of disease and death which results from the present
system of burial in earth, is infinitely larger than the evil
caused by secret poisoning is or could be, even if the
practice of the crime were very considerably to increase.
Further, the appointment of officers to examine and
certify in all cases of death would be an additional and
very efficient safeguard.   But—and here I touch on a
very important subject—is there reason to believe that
our present precautions in the matter of death-certificate
against the danger of poisoning are what they ought to
be?   I think that it must be confessed that they are

defective, for not only is our system inadequate to the
end proposed, but it is less efficient by comparison than
that adopted by foreign governments.   Our existing
arrangements for ascertaining and registering the cause
of death are very lax, and give rise, as we shall see, to
serious errors.   In order to attain an approach to certi-
tude in this important matter, I contend that it would
be most desirable to nominate in every district a properly
qualified inspector to certify in all cases to the fact that
death has taken place, to satisfy himself as far as possible
that no foul play has existed, and to give the certificate
accordingly.   This would relieve the medical attendant
of the deceased from any disagreeable duty relative to
inquiry concerning suspicious circumstances, if any have
been observed.   Such officers exist throughout the large
cities of France and Germany, and the system is more
or less pursued throughout the provinces.   In Paris no
burial can take place without the written permission of
the "Médecin Vérificateur;" and whether we adopt
cremation or not, such an officer might with advantage
be appointed here.   It is not generally known that
many bodies are buried in this country without any
medical certificate at all; and that among these any
number of deaths by poison may have taken place for
anything that anybody knows.   Is it in the provinces
chiefly that this lax practice exists?   No doubt, and
more particularly in the principality of Wales.   But it
occurs also in the heart of London.   A good many
certificates of death are signed every year in London by
some non-medical persons.   In one metropolitan parish,
not long ago, which I can name, but do not, above forty

deaths were registered in a year on the mere statement of neighbours of the deceased. No medical certificate was procurable, and no inquest was held; the bodies were buried without inquiry. This practice is not illegal, and, in my opinion, it goes far to make a case for the appointment of a " Médecin Vérificateur."

It would be possible, at much less cost than is at present incurred for burial, to preserve, in every case of death, the stomach and a portion of one of the viscera, say for fifteen or twenty years or thereabouts, so that in the event of any suspicion subsequently occurring, greater facility for examination would exist than by the present method ot exhumation. Nothing could be more certain to check the designs of the poisoner than the knowledge that the proofs of his crime, instead of being buried in the earth (from whence, as a fact, not one in a hundred thousand is ever disinterred for examination) are safely preserved in a public office, and that they can be produced against him at any moment. The universal application of this plan, although easily practicable, is, however, ob-viously unnecessary. It is quite certain that no pretext for such conservation can exist in more than one instance in every five hundred deaths. In the remainder, the fatal result would be attributed without mistake to some natural cause—as decay, fever, consumption, or other malady, the signs of which are clear even to a tyro in the medical art. But in any case in which the slightest doubt arises in the mind of the medical attendant, or in which the precaution is desired or suggested by a relative, or whenever the subject himself may have desired it, nothing would be easier than to make the requisite conservation. As before stated, the existence of an official verificator would relieve the ordinary medical attendant of the case from active interference in the matter. If, then, the public is earnest in its endeavour to render exceedingly difficult or impossible the crime of secret poisoning—and it ought to be so if the objection to cremation on this ground is a valid one—the sooner some measures are taken to this end the better, whether burial in earth or cremation be the future method of treating our dead.—Sir Henry Thompson, in *Contemporary Review.*

Avant de l'exposer, nous croyons indispensable de répondre à la principale, on pourrait même dire à la seule objection présentée contre la crémation, c'est-à-dire le danger de faire disparaître les traces d'empoisonnement. M. Cadet a discuté cette question de la manière la plus satisfaisante. Il partage, comme la Commission du Conseil de salubrité, les poisons en deux catégories.

"La première, renfermant les poisons qui ne peuvent être retrouvés que dans les cendres : substances organiques, ainsi que le mercure qui est volatil, et le phosphore, ce dernier corps étant en quantité considérable dans notre organisme ; La deuxième, comprenant les poisons susceptibles d'être retrouvés : arsenic, antimoine, zinc, cuivre, plomb, etc. ; Il est inutile de s'arrêter aux poisons de la première catégorie ; car tous, excepté le mercure, ne se retrouvent pas plus dans l'inhumation que dans la crémation."

M. Cadet examine ensuite la seconde catégorie et prend pour exemple le poison le plus connu, l'arsenic.

Il rend compte de nombreuses expériences par lui faites sur des animaux qu'il a empoisonnés par l'arsenic, et qu'il a ensuite incinérés. Il a retrouvé l'arsenic dans les cendres. La société ne serait donc pas désarmée vis-à-vis de tentatives criminelles. M. Cadet ajoute des réflexions extrêmement justes, que nous croyons devoir transcrire, parce qu'elles élucident la question de la manière la plus péremptoire.

" Quand même les poisons ne seraient pas retrouvés dans les cendres, est-ce que cette objection, quoique sérieuse, faite au nom de la médecine légale, que la crémation entrave les investigations de la justice, dans certains cas de crime, est-ce que cette objection, dis-je, pourrait être un obstacle ? Elle impose tout simplement la nécessité de prendre des précautions telles, que tout individu tenté de commettre un empoisonnement, ait à réfléchir avant de consommer le crime. Ne peut-on pas établir un mode plus rigoureux de constatation des décès ? Une enquête sévère ne pourrait-elle pas être faite avant de délivrer le permis d'incinération d'un cadavre ? Un certificat du médecin qui aura donné les soins, constatant la nature de la maladie ; un certificat du pharmacien, sur lequel seront transcrites les prescriptions du médecin, pendant la maladie ; un certificat du médecin chargé de la vérification des décès, indiquant dans quel état il a trouvé le cadavre, avec les signes qui lui sembleraient extraordinaires ; le tout envoyé à un médecin contrôleur, seraient des garanties supérieures à celles exigées aujourd'hui pour l'inhumation. En cas de mort subite ou de mort résultant d'un accident ou d'une maladie quelconque, pendant laquelle aucun médecin

n'aura été mandé pour donner ses soins, le médecin vérificateur fera une enquête dans la maison du décédé, soit
près des parents, soit près des voisins, constatera
exactement, dans son certificat, tous les renseigne-
ments recueillis, et avisera de suite le médecin contrôleur.   Si, dans la visite de ce dernier, il s'élevait
le moindre soupçon, un ordre de s'opposer à la
crémation serait envoyé à qui de droit, et le Parquet
prévenu du fait.   Que peut-on exiger de plus?   Toutes
les précautions exigées en cas d'empoisonnement ne
sont-elles pas suffisantes?   Puis, pendant la maladie, ne
pourrait-on pas exiger du médecin, chaque fois qu'il re-
márquerait des symptômes douteux ou suspects, qu'il
appelât en consultation un ou deux confrères, et après
examen sérieux, si le doute persistait, qu'il prévînt la
justice?   Et les matières vomies ne devraient-elles pas
être recueillies?   Dans de telles circonstances, l'autopsie
serait faite ; les viscères, le foie, les organes utiles pour
l'analyse chimique, seraient conservès ; puis, apres un
examen attentif de la part du medécin, le corps serait
brûlé.   Il est bien entendu que, sur la demande d'un
des membres de la famille, ou sur les désirs manifestés
par le décédé pendant sa maladie, ou sur les moindres
soupçons ou indices d'une personne quelconque, l'autopsie
aurait lieu de droit."

Voilà un ensemble de précautions parfaitement propre
à rassurer.   La crémation étant autorisée, la police, en
vertu des attributions qu'elle possède, et sans qu'il y ait
besoin de lois nouvelles, userait de son droit de faire des
règlements sur les formalités à remplir.   Elle pourrait,
dans les cas douteux, prescrire l'autopsie.   Mais cette

opération laborieuse et dispendieuse ne serait pas la
règle générale; car il y a toujours une infinité de cas
où la cause de la mort est parfaitement connue et où,
par conséquent, la crémation ne présente aucun incon-
vénient Pour obvier au danger signalé par la Commission d'hygiène, d'enlèvement ou d'altération des
cendres, on pourrait exiger que chaque urne fût scellée
et conservée dans le cimetière, pendant plusieurs années ;
de manière qu'on ne pourrait y porter atteinte sans commettre le délit de violation de sépulture.—*Rapport au
Conseil Municipal de Paris*, 1879.

THE STATE OF OUR GREAT SUBURBAN
CEMETERIES.

The greater portion of the public probably
suppose that the forbidding of burials within the
town has saved us from all present danger. The
following concerns cemeteries in the immediate
suburbs of London—some of those situated in
the most pleasant, and which will soon be
crowded, suburbs of London.

During the time that the merits of cremation have
been under discussion its advocates might have strength-
ened their case had they been cognisant of the way in
which two of the cemeteries of South London were being
managed. We refer to the Battersea Cemetery, controlled by a Burial Board elected by the Vestry of
Battersea ; and to the Tooting Cemetery, managed by a
Burial Board elected by the Vestry of Lambeth. The

Tooting Cemetery is not in the parish of Lambeth, but is in the parish of Tooting Graveney, which is comprised within the district of the Wandsworth Board of Works; and the Battersea Cemetery abuts upon the district of the Wandsworth Board. Therefore, the members of the Wandsworth Board are concerned, on behalf of their constituents, in the sanitary condition of both cemeteries. In this matter at least the multiplicity of local authorities has not been without its advantages, for it has required the action of the Wandsworth Board to put a stop to the violation of the Secretary of State's regulations in both cemeteries.

In April and May an impression prevailed among those resident near the Battersea Cemetery that an exceptional amount of sickness in the neighbourhood, including cases of scarlet fever and diarrhœa, was due to the overcrowded and consequent insanitary condition of the burial-ground. Whatever the cause of the sickness, its existence was a fact. The medical officer of health for West Battersea, Dr. Oakman, reported to the Wandsworth Board that the overcrowding also was a fact, and that it was assuming dangerous and alarming proportions. The Home Office was communicated with, Mr. Holland held an inquiry, and all that had been alleged was proved or admitted. The only person responsible in such a case for the violation of the law is the superintendent of the cemetery, who may be fined for every proved offence. In this instance, his resignation was required by the Home Office. He has suffered for the sins of himself and his Board, and has been superseded : and under the management of his successor, it is hoped that the regulations of the Secretary of State are being observed.

A description, in the London weekly organ of the Presbyterians, of a Sunday funeral at Tooting Cemetery, first directed attention to that burial-ground. It was an Irish Catholic funeral, and the mourners lowered the coffin. That was an unusually long one, and, being slightly tilted, it stuck fast half-way down the grave. A grave-digger touched it with his feet, or stood upon it, and some excitement ensued. The object of the writer was to furnish reasons for the discontinuance of Sunday funerals. Incidentally, he mentioned circumstances which pointed to illegalities in the conduct of funerals and to the overcrowding of the ground. The article was read in the Lambeth Vestry. The burial Board instituted an inquiry into what happened on the Sunday, but ignored the suggested illegalities. They sent a letter to the Vestry declaring the article to be sensational and untrue. The Vestry appointed a committee to inquire into the ignored charges. The Clerk to the Board and the Superintendent of the Cemetery being examined as witnesses, made a clean breast of it, and admitted everything. The Vestry Committee reported unanimously that every charge was established.

The irregularities at both the Battersea and the Tooting Cemetery have been of a similar character. In both cases the object was to economise ground and keep down current expenses. The length of time a burial-ground will be available is a mere question of figures if the graves are to be of a certain depth, if there is to be a foot of earth between each coffin, and if no coffin is to be within three or four feet of the top. Dr. Oakman, in his Report on the Battersea Cemetery, concludes that, if all regulations are to be carried out, it does not contain sufficient space for a year's burials, and in another part, that it must be closed in three years. This contingency it was which led the Board, with ground drained to the depth of 8 feet, to permit *graves to be dug deep enough to hold the coffins of 14 adults or 26 children. The percolation of water into these common graves produced decomposition before the graves were filled; and the emanations from them endangered the health of the clergymen and the mourners at each successive funeral up to the 14th or the 26th, as the case might be.* However, as the Board have sacrificed their manager, it may be hoped that these irregularities are things of the past at Battersea.

With regard to Tooting Cemetery, what the Wandsworth Board did was to appoint Mr. D. C. Noel, medical officer of health for Streatham and Tooting, and Mr. James Barber, the surveyor for the district, to inquire and report. The soil is gravel and clay, the latter predominating; and it therefore retains water. One day, on making a visit, they saw a coffin exposed in a private grave; it had been laid bare at the request of a family for a member of which the grave had been re-opened. The head of the coffin was immersed in one or two inches of black offensive water. *It was intended to place the next coffin immediately upon that exposed, so that a greater number could be buried in the grave.* Messrs. Noel and Barber addressed a series of questions to the Lambeth Burial Board, and these were frankly answered.

In this case, too, the ground is drained to the depth of 8 feet. One question was, " Is the under-drainage such as to prevent the accumulation of water in graves?" The answer is, "As far as possible." Another question was, " What is the greatest depth to which graves are dug?" The answer is, "Generally 12 feet, but in some few cases 14 feet." Messrs. Noel and Barber infer from these answers that there is no deep under-drainage. The material regulations affecting this cemetery are that there is to be a foot of earth between each coffin, 4 feet above the top coffin, and no second interment in an earthen grave on the same day unless it be of a member of the same family. The object of the last requirement as it affects common graves, is, that time may be allowed for the deposit of a foot of earth, "which shall be closely rammed down, never to be again disturbed." It used to be required that graves should be filled up, but the stringency of this regulation was relaxed by the provision that *if a foot of earth were closely rammed down over a coffin, the grave might be available the next day and on each succeeding day until it had received the proper number of coffins to leave the last 4 feet from the surface.* Messrs. Noel and Barber do not seem to have noticed this. The questions and answers bearing upon these regulations are as follow :—"Are several coffins buried in one grave on the same day or during the same week?" —"Yes." The offence here is in the second interment on the same day ; and it was admitted before the Vestry Committee that two interments on the same day were usual, and sometimes there were three. " Is any layer of earth placed between the coffins in the same common

grave, and what thickness?"—"*Hitherto from* 4 *inches
to* 6 *inches, but now one foot.*" "What is the greatest
number of persons over 12 years of age in one common
grave?"—"Up to the present time, six; but now, as a
foot of earth is placed between each coffin, only four."
"What is the greatest number under 12 years of age?"
—"Ten up to the present time; but, as a foot of earth
is to be placed between each coffin, there will only be
seven." It is stated, in answer to one question, that
six are the greatest number of coffins buried in a family
grave; and the extreme depth of any grave is said, in
another answer, to be 14 feet; whereas, to place one foot
of earth between each coffin and to place 4 feet of earth
between the last coffin and the surface of the ground
would require that the grave should be originally at
least 15 feet deep, instead of only 12 feet or 14 feet.
Messrs. Noel and Barber find, in conclusion, as the
Vestry Committee found before them, that the regulations have been violated; but they have apparently
fallen into an error in supposing that this cemetery was
subject to the regulation which requires that any and
every grave shall be filled up after one interment. They
report that the ground is not drained to such a depth
and in such effectual manner as shall prevent the
accumulation of water in any grave therein, *and that a
layer of a foot of earth has not been left over a previously
buried coffin.*

As the municipal government of the Metropolis is
under discussion, it may not be inappropriate to point
out that, although the Vestry elects the members of a
Burial Board, and the Vestry votes the money required

by the Board, the Vestry has no control over the Burial
Board, the members of which are practically irrespon-
sible. When the Committee of the Lambeth Vestry
asked for the attendance of the clerk to the Burial Board
and its superintendent at the cemetery, it was found
that they were unable to comply with the request without the consent of the Board. The consent was given,
but not without a protest against a resolution passed by
the Committee, and with the proviso that the permission
was not to be treated as a precedent, because the Burial
Acts did not authorise the interference of the Vestry
in the functions of the Board.

The enforcement of the law and of the existing regulations will, it is said, necessitate an appeal to the Home
Secretary for some relaxations in the case of the metropolitan cemeteries, most of which it is broadly insinuated
by the delinquent Boards have been guilty of the same
practices. There is something startling in local Boards
urging their deliberate breach of well-considered laws as
a reason why those laws should be amended. The
absorbent properties of soils, the progress of decomposition in different soils, the emanation and diffusion
of poisonous gases, the risks of mourners and of adjoining residents, are all elements which have determined
the present state of the law, and what is based on
scientific fact and experience cannot be changed, to the
detriment of the living, for the sake of enabling a local
Board to pursue a policy of so-called economy.—*Times*,
November 17, 1874.

After reading the foregoing passages in italics

G

no one can say the *fosse commune* of Paris, abominable as it is, is the worst example of the burial of the poor. Do the public, and particularly the women of England, know and acquiesce in the fact that human bodies are stacked, one over the other, with from four inches to a foot of soil between them?

The *Pall Mall Gazette* of the following day contained the following :—

Mr. Holland, the Government Inspector of Burial Grounds, held an official inquiry yesterday into certain allegations which had been made respecting the management of Tooting Cemetery, and the way in which bodies were interred. The most serious charge was that the Cemetery Board had never adopted any measures for the sufficient drainage of the cemetery. A very insufficient system of mere surface drainage was, it had been stated, all that had been provided, and in one case, at least, a coffin had been placed in a grave with water in it sufficient to cover the head of it. This was admitted by the Cemetery Board, the chairman of which, Mr. Robert Taylor, explained that the more efficient drainage of the ground had been under consideration, and that communications had been in progress for the past eight years. Mr. Holland remarked that communication with the main drainage was what was required, and said that unless some steps were speedily taken in the matter the closing of the cemetery would probably be the result.

In the course of the enquiry it was elicited that the entire drainage of the cemetery was conducted into a neighbouring ditch, which discharged itself into the river Wandle, from which many of the inhabitants in its vicinity were accustomed to draw supplies of water.

After such facts one can sympathise with the declaration of the Rev. Brooke Lambert, in a lecture at Tamworth, that the whole process is, from beginning to end, revolting and disgusting. Such a revolution in our burial arrangements will not come suddenly, but perhaps a little reflection may serve to convince those who have feelings of repulsion to urn-burial, that, as a matter of fact, less dishonour is done to the remains of those whom one loves in subjecting them to a fire which reduces them to ashes which can be carefully preserved, than in allowing them to become the subjects of the loathsome process of corruption first, and then subjecting them to the chance of being ultimately carted away to make room for some metropolitan or local improvement.

Few would not say as much who knew the shocking realities of the cemetery, but those connected with such places do all in their power, for obvious reasons, to keep the painful facts as much concealed as possible from the public. According to the *Times* report, quoted above, a mere incidental allusion in a class paper was what called attention to such a disgraceful and repulsive state of things. And yet we have a Government Inspector of Burials !

A correspondent of *Land and Water*, E. N. R., sent to that journal the following :—

How we Burn our Dead Poor.—Emerging a few days ago from the dismal recesses of a metropolitan railway-station, I chanced to ask my way of an intelligent young fellow who was going in the same direction, and who cheerfully undertook to conduct me. Having, after some consultation, decided the great question of the weather, past, present, and to come, I casually directed his attention to a large cemetery on our right—one of those huge metropolitan burial-grounds established originally far away enough from the haunts of men, but now surrounded by dwellings and closely overlooked by many hundred families.

To my astonishment I found I had touched a very familiar chord, for my guide, though not himself following the profession, had an intimate connection with the grave-digging interests, his father having "worked" in that particular cemetery for three-and-twenty years. It was really with the enthusiasm of a man who knows his subject that he imparted to me the inner working life of the Necropolis, first drawing the broad distinction between the "privates" and the "commonses," alluding almost with pathos to the sacred soil devoted to the former, and detailing with professional *sangfroid* the management of the ground dedicated to the latter.

It is scarcely worth while to reproduce the suburban vernacular in which his remarks were clothed, but he spoke like one who had seen something worth seeing when he exclaimed, " You should go in there of a night, sometimes, Sir, and see them burning the bones and the coffins. You see, they dig up the 'commonses' every twelve years (of course they dare not interfere with the 'privates '), and what they find left of them they burn."

The minute particulars of this exhumation and the subsequent cremation were described with a particularity of detail which I am sure I need not attempt; but the moral I draw from this little tale is, that if the poor are to be subjected to cremation at all, surely it would be at least as well to do it in the first instance, and to do it decently, as to postpone the operation for twelve years, and then allow it to be done anyhow !

To put the matter quite plainly : a corpse buried in 1862 is dug up to-day (in 1874) and burned, very properly; and apart from the miasmatic exhalations of the grave there is an end of it ; but, admitting that the earth was virgin ground then, it has now been thoroughly   ,.., and its disinfecting powers having been largely exhausted, a new corpse, forsooth, is placed in the old grave to tenant it for a new term !

This is a state of things deserving very serious consideration, for it is clear that it cannot go on without fatal results from a sanitary point of view, for such plans as these are only subterfuges—and, I submit, very im-

proper ones—which serve to shelve the great and press-
ng question for a time.

EVIDENCE AS TO POLLUTION.

"We," say the reporters of the Sanitary Commission, " may safely rest the sanitary part of the
case on the single fact, that the placing of the
dead body in a grave and covering it with a few
feet of earth does not prevent the gases generated
by decomposition, together with putrescent matters which they hold in suspension, from penetrat-
ing the surrounding soil, and escaping into the
air above and the water beneath."

After supporting this statement by illustrations
of the enormous force exercised by gases of decomposition, in bursting open leaden coffins
whence they issue without restraint, the reporters
quote the evidence of Dr. Lyon Playfair to the
following effect :—" I have examined," he says,
" various churchyards and burial-grounds for the
purpose of ascertaining whether the layer of earth
above the bodies is sufficient to absorb the putrid
gases evolved. The slightest inspection shows
that they are not thoroughly absorbed by the soil
lying over the bodies. I know several church-

yards from which most fetid smells are evolved ;
and gases with similar odour are emitted from the
sides of sewers passing in the vicinity of churchyards, although they may be more than thirty
feet from them."

. . . He goes on to estimate the amount of
gases which issue from the graveyard, and esti-
mates that for the 52,000 annual interments of
the metropolis (a number which has already
reached 80,000 in 1873, so rapid is the increase
of population. The above was written in 1849),
no less a quantity than 2,572,580 cubic feet of
gases are emitted, "the whole of which, beyond
what is absorbed by the soil, must pass into the
water below or the atmosphere above." The
foregoing is but one small item from the long
list of illustrative cases proving the fact that no
dead body is ever buried within the earth without
polluting the soil, the water, and the air around
and above it : the extent of the offence produced
corresponding with the amount of decaying
animal matter subjected to the process.

But "offence" only is proved ; is the result
not only disagreeable but injurious to the living ?

The report referred to gives notable examples

of the fatal influence of such effluvia when en-
countered in a concentrated form ; one being that
of two gravediggers who, in 1841, perished in
descending into a grave in St. Botolph's Churchyard, Aldgate.   Such are, however, extremely
exceptional instances ; but our reporter goes on
to say that there is abundant evidence of the injurious action of these gases in a more diluted
state, and cites the well-demonstrated fact that
" cholera was unusually prevalent in the immediate
neighbourhood of London graveyards."   I cannot
cite, on account of its length, a paragraph by Dr.
Sutherland, attesting this fact ; while the many
pages detailing Dr. Milroy's inspection of numerous
graveyards are filled with evidence which is quite
conclusive, and describes scenes which must be
read by those who desire further acquaintance
with the subject.

Dr. Waller Lewis reports the mischievous
results of breathing the pestiferous air of vaults,
and the kind of illness produced by it.   His long
and elaborate report of the condition of these
excavations beneath the churches of the metropolis,
presents a marvellous view of the phenomena,
which, ordinarily hidden in the grave, could be

examined here, illustrating the many stages of decay ; a condition which he describes as a " disgrace to any ' civilisation.' " But it may be said all this is changed now; intramural interment no longer exists ; why produce these shocking records of the past ?

Precisely because they enable us to know what it is which we have only banished to our suburban cemeteries ; that we may be reminded that the process has not changed ; that all this horrible decomposition, removed from our doors—although this will not long be the case, either at Kensal Green or Norwood, to say nothing of some other cemeteries—goes on as ever, and will one day be found in dangerous vicinity to our homes.

STATE OF COUNTRY CHURCHYARDS.

To return to our reporters ; we have seen the condition of graveyards in towns, but it will not be undesirable to glance at the evidence relating to the condition of provincial churchyards, where, in the midst of a sparse population, the pure country air circulates with natural freedom— numbers of such spots are mentioned—let one single example be " Cadoxton Churchyard, near

Neath." Respecting this, the reporter writes :—
"I do not know how otherwise to describe the
state of this churchyard than by saying that it is
truly and thoroughly abominable. The smell from
it is revolting. I could distinctly perceive it in
every one of the neighbouring houses which I
visited, and in every one of these houses there
have been cases of cholera or severe diarrhœa."
This is not a selected specimen, some are even
worse ; for further examples, see the report of Mr.
Bowie, describing graveyards at Merthyr-Tydvil,
Hawick, Roxburghshire, Greenock, and other
places.—Sir H. Thompson.

At a vestry meeting at East and West Looe, Corn-
wall, the chairman, the Rev. H. Mayo, Vicar of Talland,
described the state of the churchyard at Talland, which
is the burial-place for West Looe. Over 8000 bodies
had been interred, he said, in a little more than half an
acre of ground. The usual depth of graves was about
4½ feet deep, deeper graves being out of the question,
owing to the friable nature of the soil, which was being
continually turned over. There are no spaces between
the graves, and whenever a person had to be buried the
remains of others had of necessity to be disturbed. The
sexton had a curious mode of determining whether or
not he would be safe in opening any particular spot.
He drove a long iron bar down to the requisite depth,

and if he met with no substantial obstacle the grave
was dug. Only last week, the chairman said, he saw a
woman beside a newly-opened grave in bitter distress,
because the remains of one dear to her had been ruth-
lessly dug up and exposed. The repeated burials had
raised the soil to such an extent that the church appeared
to be in a pit, and the polluted atmosphere rendered
the sacred edifice unfit for public service. There was
constantly oozing from the graves in the higher part of
the yard a horrible slime, which came on the floor of the
belfry. He was obliged to keep disinfectants for the
safety of the ringers. Fresh primroses, which were
gathered and placed in the church for decoration on
Easter Saturday, were almost black by the following
evening, and a scientific friend had told him it was owing
to the presence of sulphuretted hydrogen in the atmosphere, in such quantities as would endanger human life.
On Ash Wednesday so fœtid was the air in the church
that the congregation was obliged to withdraw. Under
these circumstances it is not surprising that Dr. Holland,
the Government Inspector, is of opinion that something
must be done to provide a cemetery for the united town-
ships; the ratepayers, however, are determined to put
off the evil day of spending money as long as possible,
and a motion in favour of taking steps for the formation
of a Burial Board was defeated.—*Times*, 1874.

STATE OF FOREIGN CEMETERIES.

A SPANISH CEMETERY.—There is a little walled-in spot of sandy, rocky ground, some two miles outside the town from which I write—it is the cimenterio, where at last the bones of the Spanish peasant are laid in peace, waiting for the touch of that magic wand which one day is to make all things new. I entered that sacred ground a few nights since for the first time. Much as I had heard of the beauty of burial-yards abroad, I looked at least for decency and cleanliness. The first thing that struck me as I opened the gate and took off my hat was the sickly, putrid smell, that well-nigh caused me to vomit. Close before me, on a rough hewn and unlettered stone, stood two tiny coffins; the lids (always of glass) were not screwed down. I pushed one aside, and there, beautiful even in death, were the rich tresses and pink cheeks of a child of some eight summers. The other was the coffin of an infant. Both bodies were wrapped, as is customary here, in coloured silver paper—for the clothes are *burnt* invariably, as they might be a temptation to some dishonest person to exhume the coffin from its shallow grave. Just then I looked down, and lo! the whole place was covered with human bones, lying on the surface. The evening breeze rose and fell, coming from the distant Sierra Morena, and wafted to my feet—it *clung around* my feet —a light loose mass of long and tangled hair. Stooping down to look, I saw that there was plenty of it about; on the gravestones, and around the dry thistles, which grew in abundance, it twined and clung. There was no

grass, no turf—only sand, and rocks peeping out. This
then, was the end of life's brief drama here : the rude
end of a still ruder life ! I saw no tombstones worthy
of the name. I asked the old gravedigger when would
he bury the two little coffins ? "Manana" (to-morrow),
he answered ; "but the place is so full, I hardly know
where to scrape a hole."

Just then I heard the strains of martial music coming
near. A civil funeral came, heralded by its band ; and
as the shades of evening fell one more coffin was
deposited on the rude blocks of stone, to wait until the
morrow's dawn.—From " Spanish Life and Character in
the Interior during the Summer of 1873," in *Macmillan's
Magazine.*

Similar unpleasant scenes may be witnessed
in many of the fairest mountain districts of Europe,
where, notwithstanding thousands of acres of Italy
and Switzerland lying waste around, the bones
are dug up and exposed for no other " reason "
than " want of room " !

THE CEMETERIES OF PARIS.

This nuisance; in various ways bound up with
superstition, is unseen in France, but, to any one
accustomed to associate cemeteries with gardens
more or less beautiful, the cemeteries of Paris
are far from being agreeable. In these, human

love does not fail in its testimony; but such are
the evils of overcrowding, of still following plans
less evidently wrong when the city was much
smaller, and of the odious system of using the
same ground for interments many times over—
that the best aspects of these cemeteries are
painful. Nothing more agreeable is to be seen
than crowded stones, and whole acres covered
with decaying blackened "immortelles." In the
portions devoted to the graves of the rich, or of
such as passed on their way to the grave by the
paths of fame or glory, a little chapel or a
ponderous tomb often prevents for a time the
dust of individuals from mingling with the
common clay of their neighbours, and the earth
is not used merely as a deodorising medium, as
in other parts of the same cemetery.

Where the poorer people bury their dead in
this part of the graveyard may be seen a most
revolting mode of sepulture. A very wide
trench or fosse is cut, broad enough to hold two
rows of coffins placed across it, and one hundred
yards or so in length. Here they are rapidly
stowed in one after another, close together, no
earth between the coffins, and wherever the

coffins, which are very fragile, happen to be short, so that a little space is left between the two rows, those of children are placed in lengthwise between them to economise space ; the whole being done much as a workman would pack bricks together. This is the fosse commune, or grave of the humble class of people, who cannot afford to pay for the ground. The remains of these people thus dishonoured are not even allowed to rest in the grave, such as it is, but after the lapse of a short time their bones are dug up and the ground prepared for another " crop." A cutting, 13 to 14 feet wide, with the earth thrown up in high banks on either side, a priest standing at one part near a slope formed by the slight cover- ing thrown over the buried of that day, and, frequently, a little crowd of mourners and friends, bearing a coffin. They hand it to the man in the bottom of the trench, who packs it beside the others without placing a particle of earth between; the priest says a few words, and sprinkles a few drops of water on the coffin and clay ; some of the mourners weep, but are soon moved out by another little crowd, with its dead, and so on till the long and wide trench is full. They do not

even take the trouble to throw a little earth
against the coffins last put in, but simply place a
rough board against them for the night. Those
places not paid for in perpetuity are completely
cleared out, dug up, and used again after a few
years. The wooden crosses, little headstones, and
countless ornaments, are carted away or are thrown
together in great heaps, the crosses and consum-
able parts being generally sent to the hospitals as
fuel. The headstones from such a clearance
(when not claimed in good time by their owners)
go to make the drainage of a drive, or for some
similar end. And yet these people, who cannot
afford to pay for the ground in perpetuity, go on
erecting inscribed headstones, and bringing often
their little tokens of love, knowing well that a
few years will sweep away these, and that afterwards they cannot .even tell where is the dust of
those that have been taken from them. One day,
when in the Cemetery of Mont Parnasse, I saw
the workmen making a new road, the bottom of
which was formed of broken headstones, many of
them bearing a date four years before. These
had been placed on ground that had not been
paid for in perpetuity, and were consequently

grubbed up at the end of a few years when the
ground was required again for another series of
these disgusting interments. The plan is, however,
on the whole, more decent and less dangerous than
the London one of piling many bodies one over the
other, with a very little soil between each.

DISRESPECT AND INSULT TO THE DEAD.

A correspondent of the *Medical Times and
Gazette*, writing from Bordeaux, says :—

. . . The earth around one of the oldest churches
in Bordeaux seems to have something peculiarly antiseptic in its nature, so that the bodies buried during ages
were converted into mummies. During some alterations
at the beginning of this century these bodies were laid
bare, and instead of being decently buried again, they
were taken out of their resting-places and ranged upright,
in a row, around a crypt under the bell-tower of the
church of St. Michel. Here they constitute a disgusting
and demoralising show, which is visited by crowds of
people, and I am afraid that the clergy of the church are
not ashamed to pocket the profits. A rough fellow, with
a candle on the end of a stick, such as they have in
wine-cellars, goes round as showman. He taps and
thumps the bodies to show that they are perfectly sound,
tough like leather trunks, and not the least brittle.
"See here, gentlemen, is a very tall man ; see how
powerful his muscles must have been, and what excellent

H

calves he has now! The next is the body of a young woman. Remark the excellent preservation of her chemise, though it was buried 400 years ago; and see! it is trimmed with lace! The next, gentlemen, is a priest; you can see his *soutane* with the buttons on it. There is a woman with a dreadful chasm in her breast; she had a cancer. The next four are a family poisoned with mushrooms; observe the contortions on their faces from the *coliques* they suffered. See next a very old man with his wig still awry upon his pate. The next is a poor *misérable* that was buried alive. See how his head is turned to one side and the body half turned round, in the frantic effort to get out of the coffin, with his mouth open and gasping." (It is quite true that the attitude is singular, but it does not warrant the inference which the showman draws from it.) But enough of this disgusting mercenary exhibition of the human body in its lowest state of humiliation. If the guardians of consecrated sepulchres, in which people have paid an honest fee to be buried, are to dig them up and cart them off as in England, or make a show of them as here, why I can only say that "cremation" will gain a good many converts. Any one would prefer urn-burial to the chance of being thus made a spectacle. So good, too, it must be for the rising population, to take off the edge of any salutary horror they may feel at death and decay, or of reverence for the dead!

MALTA.—One of the chief sights of Malta is the crypt of the Franciscan Convent, in which are preserved the dried bodies of the monks. A monk, holding a lighted candle, went down before us into the vault or

crypt, into which air and a small allowance of daylight
are admitted by windows placed high up in the roof.
All round the crypt, in niches, stood the bodies of former
tenants of the convent, and a most ghastly sight they
were. Each figure was dressed in a monk's habit and
cowl, and was propped up by a wooden bar placed before
the waist. Our guide held the light close to each figure,
so that we might be able to see all the revolting details.
In one niche the still corpulent figure of a monk lolled
against the wooden bar which supported him : the jaw
had sunk, and the tongue hung out of the mouth. In
another a tall figure stood with its withered hands, like
mouldy parchment, crossed in front of it ; the brown
beard still clung to the chin, but the eyes had decayed
away, and the lips had shrunk back from the teeth,
giving the face a dreadful leering expression, greatly at
variance with the reverent attitude of the hands. The
sight of these horrible figures made me a stronger
believer than ever in the advisability of burning the dead.
I fancy even the prejudice with which public opinion
clings to the unhealthy and disgusting plan of endeavouring to preserve the bodies of the dead would receive a
slight shake on having ocular demonstration of what very
horrible things our mortal remains must become, even
under the most favourable circumstances. The old
heathen did very wisely in destroying, as far as possible,
all disgusting associations with death ;˙and surely there
is much less shock to sentiment in having the ashes of
those we have "loved and lost" carefully guarded in a
cinerary urn, than knowing that the body is lying festering below, amid all the noxious abominations of church-

yard earth.—Edith Osborn, *Twelve Months in Southern Europe.*

A correspondent of the *Times* writes from Alexandria :—

The other day, at Sakhara, I saw nine camels pacing down from the mummy pits to the bank of the river, laden with nets, in which were femora, tibia, and other bony bits of the human form, some two hundred weight in each net, on each side of the camel. Among the pits there were people busily engaged in searching out, sifting and sorting the bones which almost crust the ground. On inquiry I learned that the cargoes with which the camels were laden would be sent down to Alexandria, and thence be shipped to English manure manufacturers. They make excellent manure, I am told, particularly for Swedes and other turnips. The trade is brisk, and has been going on for years, and may go on for many more. It is a strange fate—to preserve one's skeleton for thousands of years in order that there may be fine Southdowns and Cheviots in a distant land !

ENGLISH VAULTS.—When it is necessary, as sometimes it must be, to disturb interments not older than the rest, but of a more ambitious character, the spectacles disclosed are such as to make one envy the pauper his quicker return to Dame Nature's all-teeming, all-receiving bosom. The family vaults of old parish churches are, as anybody may know, the scene of more grotesque incidents, more sacrilegious robberies, more horrible profaneness, than any spots above-ground, however open

to the every-day world. Nuisances, as they certainly
are, they suffer a Nemesis in the dishonour and contempt
they often bring on the poor remains they were designed
to protect and honour.—*Times*, Leading Article, 1874.

FUNERAL CEREMONY.

Our whole process of sepulture, with its wood and
lead coffins (only necessitated by our custom of keeping
the dead so long in our houses) and brick vaults, seems
to me almost like an insult to God and a defiance of
Nature's laws, endeavouring as we do—how vainly !—to
impede or even prevent the carrying out of those laws.

And now, Sir, one word on a subject akin to the
above, not necessarily combined with it as regards reform, though in my opinion they should go hand in
hand. I allude to the processes and operations to
which, dead and alive, we have to submit from the
moment of death to that of placing the remains in the
grave. How long, I would ask, are we to be subjected
to the tyranny of custom and undertakers? How long
are we to be smothered with flowing hatbands, scarves,
and mourning cloaks, mobbed and overpowered by
mutes, ostrich feathers, etc.? How long are we to continue to see the remains of some quiet old gentleman or
lady, who perhaps never in his or her life sat behind
anything more exalted than a small pony, drawn to
their last home by four long-tailed black horses, or some
one who, having lived unloved, dies unmourned, and is
yet attended to his grave by half a dozen hired mourners
at 5s. per day and their beer? Truly, it is all vanity

and vexation of spirit—a mere mockery of woe ; a pro-
longation and refining of misery to the really miserable,
a source of ridicule and contempt to those who are actors
or spectators ; costly to all, far, far beyond its value ;
and ruinous to many; hateful, and an abomination to all;
yet submitted to by all, because none have the moral
courage to speak against it and act in defiance of it.

LORD ESSEX.

CREMATION, NATURE'S PROCESS.

It is easily demonstrable that cremation is nature's
one only process of resolving lifeless matter into its
elements, and that under any circumstances it is but a
question whether this mode of consuming the lifeless
human body shall occupy a longer or a shorter period.
The sun is the source of all chemical change. All
chemical action is, in fact, a form of cremation. Life
itself is carried on by a process of combustion, and all
human beings are carrying on the process within them
from the cradle to the grave. When the fire which
effects this result is extinguished, we should get rid of
the body by nature's most rapid means of cremation and
burn it. Nature gets rid of fermenting, corrupting
matter by this means, and often indicates the consum-
mation she is aiming at by spontaneous combustion.

If inhumation had been nature's best process of
getting rid of dead animal and vegetable matter, we may
depend upon it that the beasts would have instinctively
buried their dead. But not only has she not implanted
such an instinct, but she has developed birds and

savage beast to feed on garbage and carrion, and by this means to cremate what would otherwise prove noxious and pestilential, by the process of digestion. Fire was always considered to be a sacred element by the ancients. It was never allowed to expire in the temples, and it still burns as an emblem of purity and intelligence before the altar. Cremation was esteemed the acceptable mode of making an offering. "I will *purge* with fire," "I will not suffer my Holy One to see *corruption*," are familiar texts. Which, then, is the greater desecration of human remains, to burn them with fire or to give them over to the earth and to a long process of slow combustion and corruption—a corruption that one instinctively revolts at, and which is too horrible to be contemplated?

Cremation insures the purity of the atmosphere and of the springs, both of which are contaminated to a frightful and incalculable extent by the present system of interment, as we shall immediately show. Data shall be given which will put the state of things resulting from this system in its most appalling light. The registered deaths in the United Kingdom for 1874 were 699,747. Taking this as an approximate annual death registry for Great Britain, and allowing ten years for the complete resolution of the body under the present mode of interment—a period, it is believed, considerably below the mark—we have in the kingdom nearly seven millions of dead bodies lying in various stages of decomposition, and giving off noxious exhalations by means of percolation to the atmosphere, and by sending down contaminating matter to the subterranean reservoirs. Calculating

for London alone, there were, in 1872, 76,634 deaths;
there are therefore, at a rough estimate, nearly a million
of human bodies festering in its immediate neighbourhood. Fortunately for the springs, some of the cemeteries are on clayey soils, and bodies interred in them
are to a certain extent locked up in their clay vaults,
only to be a source of mischief when they are opened.
Some of these graves have been described, by one who
is bound to know, as "very cesspools" of human remains,
which give forth their noxious gases whenever broken
into for the purpose of some fresh interment, as many a
mourner has experienced to his cost. Bodies, on the
other hand, which have been buried in sandy soils are
more quickly resolved, say in some six or seven years.
Interments in sandy soils, however, are more likely to
endanger the health of the living, for by percolation the
fluids contaminate the springs and the foul gases are
exhaled into the atmosphere. If human remains were
buried in quick lime their dissolution would be more
rapidly effected; but on the slightest reflection it is per-
ceived that this method is but a method of cremation.
Why not, therefore, at once adopt the more direct, complete, and rapid progress of cremation, and ensure the
purity of the air and water for the benefit of the living?
Deference should be paid to custom and to prejudice.
We would not interfere with the sanctity of the funeral
rite, nor deprive the Church of its dues. It would be a
good bargain if we could obtain the adoption of cremation at the price of double fees. It is quite possible to
have cremation with precisely the same funeral ceremonies as at present.—W. Cave Thomas, *Social Notes.*

REASONS AGAINST COFFINLESS BURIAL, OR THE
"EARTH TO EARTH" SYSTEM.

Though strongly averse to half measures on a question of such vital and universal importance, I hail with pleasure Mr. Seymour Haden's proposals concerning reform in the undertaker department as a step in the right direction, but still am inclined to go deeper and dive to the root of the evil, by maintaining the importance of a more decided change.

In the first place, I would remark that one great argument in favour of cremation is that the present poisoning of our watercourses and springs would be for ever at an end so far as our cemeteries are concerned, but that if Mr. Seymour Haden's proposals should be adopted (admirable in intention as they are), still the evil would remain, and not only remain, but be aggravated doubly—ay, trebly.

To illustrate my meaning, suppose a cemetery in which there are, say, for the sake of argument, 30 interments weekly. Under the present system, which is opposed to nature, and revolting in the extreme, the 30 bodies encased in the strong leaden or oaken prisons decompose slowly, taking years over that operation, and do not contaminate the surrounding earth or springs or vitiate the air in at all a sudden manner.

But turn now to the other picture ; look at it in the new light, and suppose—horrible supposition—that the 30 bodies (in which the process of decomposition has already set in while above ground), encased in some light covering, as wickerwork for instance, about as durable when compared with lead or oak as paper is to sackcloth, are fast mingling with that powerful earth, and as speedily carrying poison to our springs and along our watercourses. A change is needed, and a change is demanded, but "Heaven defend us from our friends," if we are to supply the present slow contamination of our springs by one doubly more speedy and efficacious.

Secondly, by resolving all that was mortal of one we loved into our mother earth, by means of interment in slender cases instead of leaden or oaken coffins, we effect that operation in a far speedier manner, though with the necessary delay of some years. But what need is there of any delay? Why retard nature instead of rapidly furthering her ends? I appeal to the gentler sex, whose attention has now been drawn to this vital yet depressing subject, and ask them whether, for mock sentiment's sake, the fair human body should slowly and for years go through that dreadful process, when in an hour or two, at the expense of no real sentiment (I use the expression in its loftiest and genuine sense), all that nature demands is accomplished?

"I presume no one is likely to question Mr. Seymour Haden's contention that a dead body is more quickly and innocuously resolved into its elements and assimilated, in proportion as it is brought in closer proximity with the earth. This is common knowledge. What I had hoped to see stated was how far a process of burial without coffins is likely to be less injurious to the community. Will not noxious gases still arise, and would

not water be polluted by percolation from a burial-
ground? This seems the real question at issue. Before
the body has decayed and been assimilated, is its condition not likely to be as injurious, or nearly so, as
under the present system? In every burial-ground there
would be dead bodies constantly brought in, and therefore
decay would be constantly going on. I do not yet see
how, unless people stop dying, the mere quickening of
the decay will do away with all evil results, though it may
modify their harmfulness. What I understand the
advocates of cremation to argue is that under their
system all poisonous influence would be avoided. Mr.
Seymour Haden urges as a result of his system that the
same ground might be used over and over again at
frequent intervals. To my mind it would be more
painful to dig up and destroy the graves of those we
loved, than to preserve only their ashes."—" Y " in *Times*.

The question is, will the abolition of coffins always
improve matters? The interment of the body in a mere
shroud is no new idea, and under many a lych-gate in
our old churchyards have such uncoffined corpses been
borne. Indeed it has not died out yet. In county
Kildare there resides an ancient family, the deceased
members of which are always carried to the graveyard at
Tully in this manner. It is considered in the neighbourhood to be an eccentric practice, but, nevertheless, the
family observe this peculiarity, and have done so from
time immemorial. There can be no doubt that in
ancient times the practice was almost universal amongst
those who buried their dead. It is hoped that by dis-

pensing with the coffin the body will sooner return to the elements, about which there can be no question, provided that the earth in which it is interred be a suitable one. But that is not always the case, for under certain circumstances of humidity in the soil the muscular fibres of the body are, for instance, converted into adipocere, and this substance has been even sought for to use as cart-grease. Soils which keep out the atmospheric air are nearly always favourable to the generation of this substance. Here it need hardly be stated the earth is unsuitable for sepultural purposes. The ground chosen for a cemetery may not only be too damp and clayey, and impervious to air and moisture, but it may be of too open a character. Were we to bury in light gravelly soil of this class without coffins, it is not unlikely that the foul gases would levitate faster than they ought to do. From graves with plural interments the danger would be increased. We do not know exactly why coffins were originally resorted to, but it is just possible that our forefathers discovered that in certain soils the earlier and fouler stages of decomposition proceeded at too rapid a pace for the comfort of the living. The depurative power of the soil was not equal to the strain cast upon it.

This is not an altogether theoretical statement, for an eminent foreigner has noticed that this is the case in graveyards which he had visited. A coffin may, therefore, be a desirable thing under some circumstances. It is a fit question to consider also whether it would be safe to bury the body of a man who perished (for instance) from smallpox, without protecting it by a coffin. Mischief would be less likely to result after such a lapse of time as was found necessary to destroy the coffin. Here it is where the advantages of cremation appear, for with the body is burned up all disease germs whatsoever. The thing to consider is, how many persons die from contagious diseases the germs of which not even the earth can destroy? It is not so much a question of coffin or no coffin. When the Minchinhampton churchyard was disturbed, and the black earth carted to the gardens round about, the population was simply decimated; and the same would have occurred, one would imagine, even if the coffin earth had been absent.—*Sanitary Record.*

As a man of science, we think Mr. Haden has committed the very pardonable error of trying to claim too much for his method; and the confiding reader of the first part of his letter would be led to infer that organic matter is not only incapable of putrefaction, in the ordinary sense, if buried in the earth, but that it is incapable of working any harm. The ordinary reader could infer nothing else from the following paragraph, for instance, in which the high authority of Mr. Simon is invoked by Mr. Haden :—

" Nor, again, is the effect of the earth upon fluids in a state of putrescence at all less remarkable than upon solids, filtration through a few feet of common earth being sufficient to deprive the foulest water of any amount of animal or other putrid matter contained in it. We need go no further for a proof of this than to a certain pump in Bishopsgate Street which stands opposite the rails of the old churchyard there, and of which Mr.

Simon, the distinguished medical officer of the Privy Council, gives us the following interesting account :—
'The water from this well is perfectly bright, clear, and even brilliant ; it has an agreeable soft taste, and is much esteemed by the inhabitants of the parish, though, as will be seen by the subjoined analysis, it is an exceedingly hard water . . . . (yielding carbonates of lime and magnesia, sulphate of lime, chloride of sodium, nitrates of potash, soda, magnesia, and ammonia, silica, and phosphate of lime, but of organic matter none or scarcely a trace). . . . . The quantity of nitrates in this water is very remarkable. These salts are doubtless derived from the decomposition of animal matter in the adjacent churchyard. Their presence, conjoined with the inconsiderable quantity of organic matter which the water contains, illustrates in a very forcible manner the power that the earth possesses of depriving the water that percolates it of any animal matter it may hold in solution ; and, moreover, shows in how complete and rapid a manner the process is effected. In this case the distance of the well from the churchyard is little more than the breadth of the footpath, and yet this short extent of intervening ground has, by virtue of the oxidising power of the earth, been sufficient wholly to decompose and render inoffensive the liquid animal matter that has oozed from the putrefying corpses in the churchyard.'"

The above, we are afraid, would be likely to cause a false impression, for it is a well-ascertained fact that the surest carrier and most fruitful nidus of zymotic contagion is this brilliant, enticing-looking water, charged

with the nitrates which result from organic decomposition.

What, for example, was the history of the Broad
Street pump which proved so fatal during the cholera
epidemic of 1854? Was its water foul, thick, and
stinking? Unfortunately not. It was the purest-look-
ing and most enticing water to be found in the neighbourhood, and people came from a distance to get it.
Yet there can be no doubt that it carried cholera to
many who drank it; and its analysis showed that in
composition it was very similar to the water near the
graveyard in Bishopsgate Street alluded to by Mr.
Haden. We are afraid Mr. Haden will have to confess
that at present the only known method of making organic
matter certainly harmless is the process of cremation.—
The Lancet.

Speaking of the soil, Mr. Haden says :—

It is the most potent antiseptic known . . . . it
is resolvent and re-formative as well; what under the
influence of the air was putrefaction, in the earth is
resolution; what was offensive becomes inoffensive;
what was decay, a process of transmutation. Now the
word " antiseptic " means that which opposes putrefaction.
But it is not true either that the soil is the most potent
antiseptic known, or, in a strict sense, that it is antiseptic
at all. When a body is buried naked in the soil it
putrefies, and its organic components are resolved, for
the most part, into gaseous substances. Some of those
substances are exceedingly fetid, just as they are when,
under ordinary atmospheric conditions, they are evolved

from a body putrefying above ground. When, however, the gases are made to traverse a layer of soil several feet in depth, the fetid portion of them is oxidised by the atmospheric oxygen contained in the soil, and so converted into inodorous matter, such, for example, as carbolic acid, or, what is equivalent, it is slowly burnt. Combination with oxygen is promoted by the mechanical action of porous substances like soil. Again, every drop of rain water falling upon the ground and percolating the soil contains oxygen, which in that state of solution exerts a strong oxidising action. If it were true that the soil is even a potent antiseptic in the accepted sense of the word, then it would follow that the burial of a body naked in the soil would favour its preservation. But this is exactly what Mr. Haden does not desire, though it is certainly what would result from the substitution of wickerwork coffins for those of wood, if the soil were an antiseptic. If I correctly interpret Mr. Haden's letter, one reason for his objecting to the use of ordinary coffins is that what he calls the process of transmutation—an improper application of the word when applied to such changes as he refers to—is retarded. Now, if this be the case, the evolution of gases from a body enclosed in an ordinary coffin will continue for a much longer time than from a body buried naked in the soil; and, therefore, their oxidation in the former is, *pro tanto*, more likely to be complete than in the latter.—"X." in *Times.*

Ancient Sepulchral Urn, Anglesea.

THE BISHOP OF MANCHESTER ON THE EVILS AND WASTE OF BURIAL, AND ON CREMATION.

The remarks of the Right Rev. the Lord Bishop of Manchester, made during the opening of the Social Science Congress at Manchester, October 1, 1879, are worthy of being reproduced here. He said :—

I now draw attention to the provision made in our cities for interment of the dead. On Friday last I con-secrated a portion of a new cemetery, provided by the Corporation on the south side of Manchester, fully five miles from the centre of the city, containing 97 acres, at a cost, including the land, the fencing, the laying out, and the inevitable three or four chapels, of £100,000. It is very beautiful; but two thoughts occurred to me

I

as I was consecrating the portion of it assigned to those
who desire to be buried according to the rites of the
Church of England. In the first place, this is a long
distance for the poor to bring their dead; in the second
place, here is another hundred acres of land withdrawn
from the food-producing area of the country for ever. I
do not think we always observe or calculate how much
this area is being gradually contracted by the infinite
number of works and processes, requiring space, but not
producing food, which are encroaching upon it more and
more every year; nor to what extent the power of the
country to support its population is reduced thereby.
" *Jam pauca aratro jugera regiæ Moles relinquent.*" In
times of peace and plenty we can afford to be indifferent
to this consideration; but I can easily conceive the
existence of circumstances which would make this a very
serious condition indeed. I feel convinced that before
long we shall have to face this problem, " How to bury
our dead out of our sight " more practically and more
seriously than we have hitherto done. In the same
sense in which the "Sabbath was made for man, not
man for the Sabbath," I hold that the earth was made
not for the dead, but for the living. *No intelligent faith
can suppose that any Christian doctrine is affected by the
manner in which, or the time in which, this mortal body
of ours crumbles into dust and sees corruption.* I admit
that my instincts and sentiments—the result, however,
probably of association more than of anything else—are
somewhat revolted by the idea of cremation. But they
are perhaps illogical and unreasonable sentiments. Sir
Henry Thompson has stated the case in a calm and

thoughtful paper, which shows how little ground there is for the somewhat morbid sentiments that indeed prevail in relation to the whole subject of the interment of the dead. All I call attention to is that it is a subject that will have to be seriously considered before long. Cemeteries are becoming not only a difficulty, an expense, and an inconvenience, but an actual danger.

TURKISH CEMETERIES.

The following has been sent me, since the passing of the foregoing pages through the press, by
Mr. C. W. Quin, who recently lived some years
at Constantinople :—

It is a generally accepted but erroneous notion, that
the Turks take especial pains to keep the graves of their
dead free from desecration.   Turkish cemeteries are
simply picturesque cypress woods in all their natural
wildness, not the slightest effort being made either to
cultivate or even level them.   They are generally unen-
closed, except when they are attached to mosques, or are
surrounded by houses, as in the case of the cemetery of the
Dancing Dervishes in Pera, where the famous French rene-
gade, Ahmed Pasha, the Comte de Bonneval, is buried.
There are two large cemeteries in Pera, known respect-
ively as the Grand and the Petit Champs des Morts.
They are both being gradually eaten up by the encroach-
ments of the builders and the public.   It is a painful sight
for a European to see human bones protruding from
graves which have been scratched up by the number-
less herds of wild dogs.   The Turks bury their bodies
without coffins; a single parish coffin, so to speak,
being used to convey the body to the grave.   The
body is placed in the earth in its "habit as it lived.'
The Turkish mode of burial is about the most contrary
to sanitary rules that could have been devised.   The
graves are very shallow, sometimes not more than a foot
in depth, the reason for this being that most old-fashioned

Turks still retain the superstition that the soul does not leave the body until some time after burial, when it is drawn from the grave by the Angel of Death, who would find great difficulty in performing his task if the body was buried too deeply. The consequence of this is, that in warm weather a horrible stench arises from the cemeteries. The walk from the Golden Horn to the Sea of Marmora, outside the famous Byzantine land walls, is replete with historical associations at every step of the seven miles; but it can only be taken with comfort in cool weather, the stench from the great cemetery outside the Adrianople Gate being too great to be borne. Frightful incidents are told of dogs and wolves rifling the graves of the dead; and during the severe winter of 1874-75 two wolves were found in the English cemetery at Pancaldi, outside Pera, scratching at the newly made grave of a respected member of the English colony. They had already scratched their way down to the coffin.

Iridescent Glass Cinerary Urn from Collection in British Museum.

DESECRATION OF THE WHITFIELD BURIAL-GROUND.

Here is an instance, reported in the daily papers during the last few weeks, of the fate of burial-grounds in London :—

Nathan Woolfe Jacobson, of 311 and 312 Oxford Street, was on Wednesday summoned by William Rouch, inspector of nuisances for the parish of St. Pancras, for having on 30th March removed the remains of human bodies from a portion of a disused-burial ground on the north side of the Congregational Chapel, formerly George Whitfield's Tabernacle, in Tottenham Court Road, without a licence, contrary to the provisions of the Burials Acts. These proceedings were instituted by the vestry in the interests of the public health as well as of public decency. The Rev. George Whitfield in 1756 founded a chapel or tabernacle, with a piece of ground of about half an acre attached to it as a burying-ground, and held the land upon lease. The ground was not consecrated. The lease expired in 1827, and then the ground was closed for some three years. In 1831, however, the trustees of the chapel purchased the copyhold, but in order to secure the money borrowed they mortgaged the land to a Mr. Tudor, who ultimately foreclosed, and in 1862, the land being sold by order of the Court of Chancery, the defendant became the purchaser of two-thirds of it. Now, the first interment in the ground had taken place on November 19, 1756, and the last in October 1853. The ground was used for ninety-seven years as a place of interment, and 30,000 bodies were interred in the half-acre of ground during that time. The defendant appeared to have purchased it with a view to some building speculation, and in 1863 he began to move some of the bodies from one part of the ground to the other. He was immediately summoned to that court, and fined by Mr. Knox £5, and costs. He then desisted, and allowed the ground to become the receptacle of refuse, until it became such a nuisance that the sanitary authorities proceeded to fence it in with the view of making ornamental grounds. Thereupon the defendant filed a bill in Chancery, and in February of the present year succeeded in obtaining a decree restraining them from interference. Having obtained that decree in his favour he had now resumed his attempt to excavate the ground and to disturb the remains of the dead. He thought the magistrate, after hearing the evidence, would consider the defendant's proceedings to be most indecent, and to call for his intervention.

Mr. William Rouch, inspector of nuisances, said he knew Whitfield's burial-ground, the area of which is about half an acre. He had known it thirty years. It had been closed about 1853. It was thickly studded with graves in every part, and was in a populous neighbourhood. On Tuesday he went to the ground, which was then enclosed by a high hoarding. He was refused admission, but subsequently was admitted by an order from the magistrate. He found men at work excavating the ground, and there were horses and carts being loaded. Men were digging, and earth

and human bones were being dug out together. He
saw parts of human skulls, rib bones, leg bones,
shoulder bones, etc. There were decayed pieces of
wood, which had formed parts of coffins. There were
about a bushel of human bones in a box near the
carts which were being loaded, and in a trench he
found about a cartload of human bones, which had
been previously dug out; there was only a sprinkling
of earth over them. The workmen said they had no
appointed shoot for the mould, and that they took it
to Haverstock Hill or elsewhere. He had visited the
place again on Wednesday and found the men still at
work. Four horses and carts were being loaded, and
the mould taken away through the streets.

Mr. Harston argued that the burial-place not being
consecrated it did not come within the Act, as there
had been no interments there since 1853, and the Act
was not passed till 1857. It had been so decided by
the Court of Queen's Bench in the case of *Foster and
Dodd*, and when this matter was recently before the
Master of the Rolls he said there was nothing whatever
to prevent the defendant building on it. The point
had been fought out over and over again, and had always ended in one way. I can assure you we do not
wish to make any scandal. Mr. Newton—But it is a
scandal. Mr. Harston—You must remember the Bank
of England is built on an ancient burying-ground. Mr.
Newton—I know nothing of that. Still it is a scandal
that this thing should be permitted.

VIOLATION OF THE GRAVES AT ST. DENIS.

The other day I came across a somewhat rare little brochure,—an account of the violation of the royal sepulchres of St. Denis during the first French Revolution :—

The work of destruction and sacrilege commenced early in October 1793, and lasted all the month. The first corpse found was that of Henri IV., the once beloved Henri de Navarre. Some curiosity, if not affection, still seems to have lingered even among those patriots who had constituted themselves body-snatchers, and the Bearnais was propped up against the church wall in his shroud, and became quite an attraction for the crowd. One of the Republican Guards even conde-scended to cut off the king's gray, upturned moustache, and place it on his lip; another removed the beard, which he declared he would keep as a relic. After these marks of attention were exhausted, the body was thrown into a huge pit filled with quicklime, into which suc-cessively followed those of its ancestors and descendants.

On the next day the corpses of Henri IV.'s wife, Marie de Medecis, that of his son Louis XIII., and that of his grandson Louis XIV. were added to this. The body of the Sun King (as Louis XIV.'s courtiers loved to call him) was as "black as ink." What a contrast to that majestic, bewigged head, as we see it on the canvas of Le Brun and Rigault, must not that poor blackened skull have been! The body of the Grand Monarch's wife and that of his son the Dauphin (father of Louis XV.) followed. All these, and especially the latter, were in a state of shocking decay.

The following day poor harmless Marie Leczinska's body was torn from its resting-place, as also were those of the "Grand Dauphin," the Duke of Burgundy and his wife, and several other princes and princesses of the same race, including three daughters of Louis XV. All these were in a state of terrible decomposition, and in spite of the use of gunpowder and vinegar the stench was so great that many of the workmen were seized with fever, and others had to continue the gruesome work. By a strange chance, on the very morning that Marie Antoinette's sufferings came to an end on the Place de la Révolution, the body of another unfortunate queen again saw the light of day—it was on the 16th of October that the body of our Queen Henrietta Maria, who had died in 1669, was taken from its coffin and added to the ghastly heap in the "ditch of the Valois," as the pit into which these royal remains were hurled was called; that of her daughter, the once "Belle Henriette," came next; and then in quick succession the bodies of Philippe d'Orleans; that of his son, the notorious Regent; of his daughter, the no less notorious Duchesse de Berri; of her husband, and half-a-dozen infants of the same family. On the same day a coffin was cautiously opened. This was found at the entrance of the royal vault (the customary position for that containing the latest deceased king), and contained the remains of Louis "le bien aimé." No wonder that the body-snatchers hesitated before withdrawing the corpse from its enclosure, for it was remembered that Louis had perished of a most terrible illness, and that an undertaker had died in consequence of placing the already pestilent corpse in its coffin. Consequently, it was only on the brink of the ditch that the body was removed and hastily rolled over the edge; but not without the precaution of discharging guns and burning much powder, and even then the air was terribly tainted far and near.

I turn the page and find that we are only in the thick of all these dead men's bones and uncleanness, for the Republican Resurrectionists began by the Bourbons and had still to disentomb all the Valois, and further back, up to the Capetian line, and are not content until the almost legendary remains of Dagobert and Madame Dagobert 'reappear. Suffice it to add, that after Louis the Well-Beloved had been disposed of, came in succession, like the line of royal ghosts seen by Macbeth, Charles V., who died in 1380, whose body was one of the few well preserved, and was arrayed in royal robes, with a gilt crown and sceptre, still bright; that of his wife, Jeanne de Bourbon, who still held in her bony hand a decayed distaff of wood; Charles VI. with his Queen, Isabeau de Bavière; Charles VII. and his wife, Marie d'Anjou; and then Blanche de Navarre, who died in 1391. Charles VIII., of whom nothing but dust remained, Henri II., Catherine de Medecis, Charles IX., and Henri III. were disinterred on the morning of the 18th; "after the workmen's dinner," Louis XII. and his queen; and among other less interesting royal remains, the bones of Hugues, Comte de Paris,

father of Hugues Capet. And so on the work went, till
one tires even of the details of the preservation of this or
that king and queen. Can anything be more shocking than
to know that all the horrors of decay and decomposition
will remain even after two or three centuries have passed
over the lifeless form, and that, supposing one has the
ill-luck to be thus coffined and one's body removed, "a
black fluid, emitting a noxious smell," will run from out
our last home, as was the case with those Royal remains
during that hot summer month at St. Denis in 1793?—
Lord Ronald Gower in *Vanity Fair*.

Who, after reading such instances, can doubt
that it is infinitely better that the dead should be
quickly resolved into white and odourless ashes,
than subjected to insult and degradation even
much less shocking than the cases mentioned in
the foregoing pages? Some pretend that they do
not care what becomes of their bodies after death,
but a healthier feeling would make us determine
that all such horrors, as disgraceful to the living
as disrespectful to the dead, should be impossible
now and for ever.

A CONTRAST: BURIALS IN CHINA AND JAPAN.

The following note has been sent me by Mr. Maries, who has recently spent several years in China and Japan. It throws some light on the question treated of in the previous pages, in the comparison between two populous countries, one practising burial and the other cremation :—

In the country, near Shanghai, the land is a continuous graveyard. Everywhere, almost in every field, are graves in mounds of earth, or coffins standing exposed on four legs. I believe these remain for some time exposed, and are afterwards buried or set on the ground, and a large mound piled over them, 2 feet to 5 feet high and 7 feet through. All round the walls of Ichang is this graveyard, notwithstanding that the land for agricultural purposes is valuable, and there is a dense population. There are always dozens of dogs in these cemeteries. I saw once, at Ichang, these brutes devouring the body of a boy, who had been buried a day or two before in a coffin not sufficiently strong, and with only a few stones put on the top of the lid. Many such horrible sights are seen by travellers in various parts of China.

I saw, just outside the town of Chinkiang, on the river Yangtse, about twenty coffins stacked on the top of each other, the coffins being only a few rough boards nailed together. The place was too horrible for anyone

to go near. There also are low hills of considerable
extent, covered with graves of men who fell in the
Taiping rebellion, each marked by a little' mound of
earth, which is covered with rough grass ; no cultivation
is attempted in the place. There are also old Man-
darins' or high officials' graves in this neighbourhood,
which take up more space. The Ming tombs at
Nangkin, where monster stone figures are set up on
each side the road leading to the tombs may be mentioned. There are smaller ones at the old warriors'
graves, with men, horses, elephants, lions, etc., in stone,
guarding the path to the graves of the old rulers or
warriors, and often taking up an enormous space of
valuable land that is uncultivated now, and the home
of pheasants and hog-deer. At Ichang I noticed a
graveyard of several miles extent, and of the most
valuable land for agriculture. Not a tree or bush was
to be seen, of any size, except at a temple.

My impressions of China are the reverse of the
pleasant ones I have of Japan. It is, in fact, so far as
I saw it, a sad and unpleasant country, and is to a great
extent made so by the very inefficient and disgusting
modes of burial one is there compelled to witness in
travelling by the roadsides or in the fields. It is also
a most costly plan to the country, as it prevents much of
the choicest land in it from producing food, or beautify-
ing the land near the cities with trees or parks.

The Japanese, on the contrary, burn their dead in
all cases, and while they thus save their land for the use
or pleasure of the living, their cemeteries are really
beautiful places. Sometimes they are placed in a

lovely valley, shaded by enormous pines, and sometimes
on little lawns or ledges on hillsides. Usually each
family using the cemetery has a small square of ground
allotted to it in which the ashes are buried.

There is, of course, a great saving of land as compared with the Chinese, or even with our own method.
Over the buried ashes .a stone, often beautifully cut,
containing the name of the family or individual, while
vases for flowers and lamps are frequently seen near
the graves in these beautiful and in no way offensive
cemeteries. The evergreen bushes used to plant in
these cemeteries are Ilicium religiosum, the Tea-shrub,
Camellias, and Euryia japonica. I have seen specimens of the Maiden Hair tree or Ghinko (Salisburia) in
these cemeteries. In the principal ones, too, may be
seen noble specimens of the Umbrella pine and other
rare trees. This desirable result is attained notwithstanding the fact that the Japanese mode of cremation
is a very imperfect one, much more so than it need be.
I speak of what I saw in villages ; but in some of the
cities a better system is in use. The Japanese are firmly
persuaded of the merits of their system.

We have now had some evidence of the great
need for burial reform, and of the state, so often
shameful, of cemeteries in many different lands.
The ideas set forth in the first part of this book
are printed in the hope that all who cherish the
memory of their dead may be led to consider the
many evils of the present system, and that they

may help to save us from the danger, the horror, and the degradation of the grave. It is for the most advanced and cultivated of the great nations of the West to lead the way in this essential reform, called for in the interest of the Living ; of beauty of open spaces in cities ; respect for the memory of the Dead, of Art, and of natural beauty.

Glass Urn, Sardinia (Henderson Collection, British Museum).

Printed by R. & R. CLARK, *Edinburgh.*

www.ingramcontent.com/pod-product-compliance
Lightning Source LLC
Chambersburg PA
CBHW021132020726
47500CB00003B/1043